Hansjörg Schneider, born in Aarau, Switzerland, in 1938, has worked as a teacher and journalist, and is one of the most performed playwrights in the German language. He is best known for his Inspector Hunkeler crime novels. *Silver Pebbles*, following on from the success of *The Basel Killings*, is the second in the series to appear in English. Schneider has received numerous awards, among them the prestigious Friedrich Glauser Prize for *The Basel Killings*. He lives and writes in Basel.

SILVER PEBBLES

Hansjörg Schneider

Translated by Mike Mitchell

BITTER LEMON PRESS
LONDON

BITTER LEMON PRESS

First published in the United Kingdom in 2022 by Bitter Lemon
Press, 47 Wilmington Square, London WC1X 0ET

www.bitterlemonpress.com

First published in German as *Silberkiesel* by Ammann Verlag, Zurich, 1993

The translation of this work was supported by the Swiss Arts Council Pro Helvetia

A CIP record for this book is available from the British Library

PB ISBN 978–1–913394–622
eB USC ISBN 978–1–913394–639
eB ROW ISBN 978-1-913394-646

Typeset by Tetragon
Printed and bound by CPI Group (UK) Ltd, Croydon CR0 4YY

swiss arts council
prohelvetia

SILVER
PEBBLES

*It's telling a story, you see, simply telling a story,
writing a picture book with the train, the house,
the street in it, the things a man sees every day, yet
doesn't see at all because they're too familiar.*

FRIEDRICH GLAUSER

The Frankfurt–Basel Intercity – a sleek, streamlined train – was crossing the Upper-Rhine plain. It was the middle of February, there were fingers of snow along the bare branches of the vines going up the slope to the east. A picture-postcard landscape dotted with crows and villages with pointed gables.

Guy Kayat, a thirty-five-year-old Lebanese in a camel-hair coat, was standing at the corridor window, the empty compartment with his reserved seat behind him; on the floor beside him was his black travel bag of African antelope leather. To steady himself he had his left hand on the lower window frame, a cigarette in his right hand. He was tired from his early-morning flight from Nicosia to Frankfurt. It had been pleasantly warm in Nicosia, the sky blue, but now the world outside was grey and cold. How could people live in that unpleasant climate, he wondered, why didn't they emigrate? For him it was no problem, he was only intending to spend a few days in Basel, he was travelling on business.

The train thundered into a tunnel and Kayat leaned back, away from the noise of the wheels. He dropped his cigarette and trod it out. Nervously he looked up and down the empty corridor: there was no one to be seen. He checked his tie, the knot was perfectly in place. Everything was as it should be, and there would be no problems with the rest of the journey.

As the train came out into the light again and the clatter of the wheels stopped, two men dressed in discreet grey appeared at the far end of the corridor. Kayat could see at once that they were officials. One of them opened the door of the first compartment and went in. The other gave Kayat what seemed to be a bored glance.

Kayat's mouth went dry. It was a familiar feeling and he knew that now he had to stay calmly by the window and wait for what was to come. It was quite normal for Swiss customs officials to check travellers to Basel, he was ready for that. Keep calm, give them a friendly smile and don't turn a hair – that, after all, was his profession.

Kayat took another cigarette out of the packet and lit it. His right hand with the lighter was trembling, his armpits had started sweating. What was all this? Why was he losing his nerve?

He inhaled deeply, then turned his head to the left, towards the men. One was clearly still in the compartment, the other standing there, legs apart, in the corridor, holding a thick, black book he'd taken out of the briefcase on the floor by his feet. He leafed through it slowly until he came to the right page, then took a pencil out of his breast pocket and made a note in it. Putting the pencil away again, he closed the book and looked along the corridor, narrowing his eyes as if something had caught his attention.

Kayat knew that, as an Arab, he stood out in this country. He was aware of how people looked at him when he walked round Frankfurt, that flash of unconscious hatred covered up at once with an insincere smile. The fact was that people were racist, here and elsewhere, even though they would never admit it. They were racist because they felt insecure in their different-coloured skin and therefore saw everything foreign as a threat. It wasn't that bad. And if you behaved correctly and always had enough money on you, then you were treated correctly, even as an Arab.

But now that the customs officer had put away his black book and was coming resolutely towards him, Kayat lost his nerve. He started coughing, as if the smoke he'd inhaled had caught in his throat. He bent over and coughed until the tears came. He trod out the cigarette, took a white hand-kerchief out of his pocket and, still coughing and almost retching, held it over his mouth, picked up his travel bag and hurried away along the corridor. When he got to the end of the carriage and could no longer be seen from the corridor, he pushed on the handle of the automatic sliding door with all his might. The sound of the train going over the sleepers and the wheels on the rails was almost deafening, and there was a dusting of snow in the gap between the two coaches. He tugged open the second door and ran on. He'd stopped coughing. He put away his handkerchief, fingers trembling. What was all this? Was he running away? But where could he go? He was on the train, it was locked, and he couldn't jump off at this speed anyway.

He yanked open the door to the restaurant car. There were only a few passengers at the tables. They looked up as he burst in – he was going much too fast for a normal pas-senger. Added to that he was soaked in sweat and his panic was surely obvious from his expression.

He stopped and tried to regulate his breathing; raising his left arm he checked his watch. Then he looked round, as if he wanted a table. Perhaps he should sit down and make himself inconspicuous, like an ordinary person on a journey, order a coffee, quietly wait for the customs officer to appear and show them his passport when they asked. It was valid, there was nothing wrong with it, there was no cause for concern.

Kayat turned round and looked at the glass door he'd just come through. Nothing was moving behind it. Out of the window he saw a wine-growing village slip past, the roofs white with snow. The people at the tables had calmed down, some were quietly dozing, others were reading magazines, no one was looking at him anymore.

When the waiter with a fat red face, clearly a southern European, came to show him to a table, Kayat made a decision. He was now quite calm, in control of the situation, however critical it might be. He thanked the waiter but said no, he didn't want a table and went out through the door at the other end of the car, gently touched the handle of the automatic door, waited until it slid open and went into the next carriage. It was a first-class carriage in bright colours that rolled almost silently along the rails.

Kayat pushed open the door of the toilet. He went in, closed it behind him and opened his travel bag. Putting his hand inside, he ripped off the false bottom that had been stuck on, threw it into the lavatory and flushed it away. Then he took out a flat plastic bag with diamonds in it. He tore open a packet of condoms, took one out and put the diamonds in. Taking a spray can of shaving cream out of a leather bag, he undid his trousers and pulled down his boxer shorts. He sprayed some foam on his hand, rubbed it on the condom and, bending down and supporting himself on the lavatory with his other hand, pushed the diamonds right up inside his rectum. He stood up straight again, ignoring the pain, and waited a while to ensure that the diamonds stayed inside. They did.

When there was a knock on the door, he pulled up his trousers, zipped them up with a precise, swift movement, sprayed shaving foam all over his chin, pulled a disposable razor out of the packet and shaved the left half of his face.

When there was a second knock, this time louder and firmer, he opened the door. The customs officer was there, a young man with a blond beard.

"May I see your passport, please?" he asked.

"Of course," Kayat said, "just one moment."

He washed his hands carefully, dried them on a paper towel, threw it in the trash and took his passport out of his jacket pocket. "There you are," he said with a friendly smile as he handed it over.

The official had watched without a word, legs braced against the rocking of the carriage. He took the passport and leafed through it, stopping at the photo, which he stared at for a long time.

"You're Lebanese," he said.

Kayat carefully shaved the foam off the right side of his face. "Yes. That's not forbidden, I presume?"

The official took a piece of equipment out of his briefcase and typed something into it while Kayat dried his face. He waited without looking up and received an answer which he clearly didn't like.

"OK," he said, "there's no record of anything against you."

"What record should there be?" Kayat asked in his best German, which seemed to confuse the young man.

"You never know, there are all sorts of people hanging around. May I?"

"Of course," Kayat said, setting his open travel bag on the toilet seat. The official lifted up a couple of shirts, felt underneath and brought out some underclothes.

"Just the kind of things one needs," Kayat said, shrugging apologetically.

"On holiday?" the official asked.

"Yes," Kayat said, "a vacation."

"And this here?" The official was holding the torn-open packet of condoms.

Kayat lowered his eyes with a guilty expression. "You never know."

"Right then," the blond official said, in a matter-of-fact tone, "you can pack everything up now." And after a pause: "Why did you run away then?"

"Coughing fit," Kayat said, "I almost spewed up."

Peter Hunkeler, detective inspector with the Basel police, formerly married with one daughter, now divorced, was stuck in the traffic jam on the Johanniterbrücke over the Rhine. It was already starting to get dark, even though it wasn't yet 4 p.m., and the Intercity from Frankfurt was due at 4.27. The cars had their lights on, their windshield wipers as well, for light snow was drifting down out of the fog. At higher altitudes, the TV weatherman had forecast, there was now good visibility as far as the Alps. Up there you could see a gleam of red in the west, where the sun was going down, to the south the snow-covered slopes were shining like the moon and the first stars would soon appear.

Peter Hunkeler was nervous. It wasn't the understandable nervousness of someone arriving late and missing an important meeting through his own fault – and the assignment at Badischer Station was hugely important. That didn't bother Hunkeler; he had been in the police too long to worry about personal failure. Sometimes an operation was successful, sometimes not. For him as an inspector the difference wasn't that great. If an operation went well, the praise of his superiors had its limits; if not, the rebuke had its limits too. Moreover, he was only a few years away from retirement and, as a state official, his pension was assured. Promotion was no longer a possibility and dismissal after so many years highly unlikely.

And what about the professional ethos of the guardian of the law, the brave fighter for justice? He couldn't care less about that, to be honest. He was fed up with that kind of prattle and had been for years. The things he'd seen in his time with the police had put paid to his youthful belief in justice.

A crime, what was that? A poor devil, in desperate straits financially and emotionally, who goes to pieces just once in his life and commits some terrible misdeed which he can't understand later on and bitterly regrets, is branded a monster by the law and convicted. A rich moneybags, who has a dozen lawyers at his beck and call and knows the law like the back of his hand, rips people off every which way for years on end – there's your worthy citizen.

And first you have to catch your criminal and convict him. Peter Hunkeler was sceptical about that. "Of course," he would say when holding forth to his fellow regulars in the bar, "of course it's easy to convict a man who kills his wife out of jealousy and goes to the nearest police station to confess. But you just try and prove that a rich gentleman who lives up there on Bruderholz in a nice villa with a swimming pool and two or three sheep in his garden has earned his millions by laundering drug money."

Hunkeler looked to the right, down through the railings of the bridge to the Rhine. There was a dull gleam on the surface of the water. The water down there was dark at this time of the year, cold water, murky water, drifting down to the sea. In the summer it was seaweed-green and warm, he loved swimming in it in the evening. Now it looked curdled. Further upstream it was crossed by Mittlere Brücke, it too crammed full of cars, and beyond it the chancel of the cathedral rose up against the evening sky, barely visible in the softly falling snow.

Hunkeler watched the wipers making triangles on the windshield. He switched off the engine, put his hands on his knees, closed his eyes and breathed calmly, repeating to himself sentences he'd learned on a free course in autogenic training put on by the Basel police. "I am calm and relaxed," he repeated in a low voice, "and my right arm is heavy and warm." He noticed how these stupid sentences were starting to take effect, how he was slipping away from the outside world to somewhere deep within his body. Before he could enter a pleasant state of suspension, he opened his eyes wide.

Nothing had changed in the meantime, except that there was a thin layer of snow on the windshield.

He was not unhappy sitting there in the traffic jam, stuck between the car behind and the one in front, waiting for something that ought to happen but never did. It was rest-ful being out of circulation, safe in the general paralysis. Hunkeler started at a honk from the vehicle behind him. He had nodded off after all, thinking about his daughter Isabelle, dreaming of the good times with her, with his beautiful, clever, cheerful Isabelle whom he hadn't seen for a year.

He looked in the rear-view mirror. The man at the wheel behind him was throwing his arms around furiously and tapping his forehead. Hunkeler gave an apologetic shrug, which only made the man more furious and sound his horn again. Hunkeler turned the engine back on and set off.

On the other side of the bridge were two cars that had crashed into each other. The policeman by the revolving blue light waved Hunkeler on.

He arrived at the station on time, parked, got out and ran onto the concourse. Detective Sergeant Madörin, who was standing at the kiosk behind a rack of newspapers, gave him an unobtrusive sign. The large hand of the clock up in the cupola – funeral-parlour architecture, Hunkeler thought – showed half past four.

He saw his men at once: Haller standing by the German Federal Railways ticket office smoking his curved pipe, Schneeberger sitting reading a book on a bench in the middle of the concourse and Corporal Lüdi studying a timetable on the wall by the exit. None of them looked across at Hunkeler, who strolled over to the kiosk to buy some cigarettes.

The first passengers started coming down the passage from the platform. The customs official let them all through: a young couple who had greeted each other with kisses and were now heading, full of anticipation, for the exit, some businessmen with briefcases who looked neither to the right nor to the left, an elderly woman who was obviously expecting to be met and stood there on the concourse, bewildered.

Then Guy Kayat appeared. Hunkeler recognized him at once, he'd studied his photo often enough: a young, powerful Arab in a camel-hair coat with a black leather bag who was walking in a strangely stiff way. He stood still for a moment, had a brief look round, then headed for the exit. A man – a bald, rather fat fifty-year-old oozing Swiss respectability – left the bank counter, where he'd clearly been changing money, turned towards Kayat, trying to give him a discreet sign, and when that brought no response, hurried over to him.

"That's him," Madörin hissed, about to dash off. Hunkeler held him back. The bald man grabbed Kayat by the arm, turning him round, but Kayat shook him off, pushed him away and said something to him they couldn't make out. The Swiss, baffled, looked round the concourse. Lüdi was already running towards them. Dropping his travel bag, Kayat grabbed the man, threw him at the charging Lüdi, then ran off, past the kiosk to the passage leading to the toilets. Hunkeler and Madörin would probably have been able to catch him had a couple with a child and a loaded luggage trolley not suddenly come round the corner, with the result that they knocked the child over and fell down themselves. Hunkeler struggled to his feet, swearing, just in time to see Kayat heading down the corridor to the men's toilet.

Madörin had also got up by now. "Police!" he shouted, pulled out his pistol and shot off down the corridor with Haller and Schneeberger.

Hunkeler gestured an apology. "I'm so sorry," he said to the horrified parents, "it's diamonds we're after. Go and report to the police." He watched the mother pick up the child and try to comfort him. Then he ran off to the toilets – after all, he was in charge of the operation and God only knew what Madörin was doing with his gun.

He arrived just in time to stop Haller, who, covered by his colleague who was holding the gun, arm outstretched, was about to break down the toilet door with his shoulder.

"Stop!" Hunkeler shouted. "Are you out of your minds?" Pausing for Madörin to move aside, disappointed, he pushed on the door handle and the door opened.

On the right of the tiled room were two wash basins, on the left four urinals; the cubicles were at the back. He knocked on the first door. It was a while before it opened. Standing there was an old man who had clearly just pulled up his trousers. He was trembling with fear.

Hunkeler was about to apologize when he noticed Madörin kicking the next door in, gun at the ready. A young man, a drug addict, the needle in the crook of his arm, was sitting on the toilet. He made no sound but his upper body sank back against the cistern and, eyes closed, his head slumped onto his chest.

The lavatory flushed in the next cubicle. The door opened and Kayat came out looking surprised to see the men, who immediately seized him. Hunkeler watched as Madörin dashed over to the toilet bowl, tore off his jacket, rolled back his sleeve and stuck his arm in up to the elbow. "Nothing," he said.

*

Erdogan Civil, thirty-eight, a seasonal worker from Selçuk in Turkey, married with three children, was showering in the Basel sewage workers' changing room in Hochbergerstrasse. Together with his foreign colleagues he'd spent six hours in the underground pipes, in the high, nine-foot-wide mains that gathered the sewage from the surrounding district, and in the narrow feeders you couldn't even stand up in. At midday he'd had a snack that he'd taken with him in a plastic bag and had drunk a bottle of beer. Now his day's work was behind him and he was rinsing off the sewer smell.

He wouldn't have said he found the smell unpleasant. What could be unpleasant about it? It was very well-paid work. In Turkey an unskilled worker like him would earn the equivalent of a hundred Swiss francs a month. Here he got thirty times as much. With wages like that he had a very good life over here and had no problem supporting his family, even with all the grandparents, aunts and sisters-in-law that he'd had to leave behind in Turkey. He was also managing to put aside two or three hundred francs a month, which in a few years would allow him to buy a small hotel with a dozen beds. Selçuk was close to the old Greek city of Ephesus. It was swarming with backpackers who came to see the ruins and needed as cheap a bed as possible. Erdogan would have all his beds occupied. If to achieve that he had to spend a few years crawling round the sewers of this cold town, it was well worth it.

In the course of his work, he had noticed that each smell developed its own dynamic. Sometimes the smell was a horrible stench that almost made you puke, but in no time at all it made you feel at home – it was familiar and comforting.

You could get used to anything, Erdogan had learned, apart from the humiliation of despair.

He squeezed some more shampoo out of the container fixed to the wall and rubbed the milky liquid into his hair, making sure none ran down into his eyes. He scrubbed his head, for that was where the sewer smell got deep into your pores, then let the warm water pour down over it, feeling the warmth spread through his body. He heard his fellow workers break out into loud laughter; they were already putting on their outdoor clothes. Erdogan was always the last out of the shower. Luigi, the Italian, had been telling another of his jokes about a woman and a randy man.

He turned off the shower and went through into the changing room, where he saw that Berger, the foreman, was standing between the two benches. He was the only Swiss in the team, not a bad boss but sometimes a bit pig-headed, the way the Swiss were. But at least he didn't make any distinction between Italians and Turks.

"You there," Berger said, looking across at Erdogan, "you'll have to go down again."

"Why me?" Erdogan asked.

"Someone has to do it," Berger said, "and you're not dressed yet."

None of the others said anything. They kept their heads down, glad it wasn't them.

"Sorry, I can't," said Erdogan. "I've got a date."

"Off you go now," Berger said. "The connection from Badischer Station is blocked, at the junction of Schwarzwaldallee and Markgräflerstrasse. Take the rod. You'll be back here in half an hour – and you'll be on overtime."

Erdogan knew there was no point protesting, so he dried himself and put his work clothes back on. He'd be late for his girlfriend Erika, but she knew that from time to time he went to see his mates in Café Ankara after work, and an hour's overtime wasn't bad, anyway.

Outside he got on his moped, put on his helmet and rode into town. It was icy cold. There was snow in the air. On the other side of the road, cars with German licence plates were heading at walking pace for the border – commuters who worked in Basel and lived in Baden.

As he drove over the River Wiese he could see that it was frozen on both sides, that the water was only flowing free in the middle. He was concentrating so much on the river that he almost drove into a truck but he managed to brake just in time and regain control of his skidding moped.

Once he was down in the Schwarzwaldallee pipe, he immediately saw what was wrong: the feed-in pipe from Badischer Station was blocked with dirty diapers, toilet paper and a bright green article of clothing whose colour made it stand out.

The usual, he thought. The women take their babies to the station toilet, change them and simply flush the dirty stuff away. Or they come into Basel from some village in the Wiese valley, buy themselves a new dress and stuff the old one down the station WC – meaning that they, the sewage workers, have to get back into their work things and clear out the mess.

Erdogan shook his head, realizing he'd sworn in Swiss German, which sounded oddly out of place in the deserted pipe. He looked around and shone his helmet lamp on the part of the pipe he'd come down. All he saw was a rat carefully licking its paws. Odd, he thought, that he wasn't swearing in Turkish anymore.

He shoved the rod up the pipe from the station, but the blockage didn't move. Sticking his hand in, he tugged at the green dress. He almost fell over backwards but managed to save himself with two quick steps. He swore again, this time in Turkish. He pushed the rod in once more, putting all his strength into it now, deeper and deeper until he saw dirty water begin to trickle out. He pushed the rod further in, more than three feet now, and pulled the whole blockage out, inch by inch. As it hit the floor of the pipe, he quickly stepped aside to avoid the torrent that followed.

Once the water had subsided, he reinserted the rod into the mess on the bottom of the pipe, pushing it into the deeper water so it would be washed away. As he did so, he noticed a torn condom, and next to it something that sparkled in the light of his helmet lamp.

The bastards, Erdogan thought, now they're even chucking glass down the toilet.

In the past he'd fished out spectacles, sometimes undamaged ones. But whatever was shining on the bottom of the pipe didn't look like a piece of a lens; it looked more like a little glassy pebble. And when he looked more closely, he saw that there were more of these little pebbles lying around.

He bent down and picked one up. It was about the size of a drop of water, with clear faceted surfaces, and once he'd rubbed it clean with his handkerchief and given it a good look in the light of his lamp, he saw that it had a glint of blue.

Startled, Erdogan wrapped it up in his handkerchief and put it in the side pocket of his waterproof overalls. Then he looked around. There was nothing to be heard but the drip,

drip, drip of the water and the distant roar of traffic above. There was no one else there apart from the rat, which was still cleaning itself up.

He could feel his heart pounding; he could feel it even in his neck. That was a diamond, that much was immediately clear to him. And down there in front of him were more diamonds. But where were the people who'd lost them?

Bending down, he poked around in the pile of waste, then he knelt and started to collect everything that glittered. He worked quickly but calmly, going through everything, turning over every piece of paper and every cigarette end. After he'd systematically gone through the pieces of green dress, he walked a little way down the sewer to see whether any had been washed down. He shone his flashlight up the feeder pipe from the station, scraped out everything that was still in it and found two more diamonds. When he was sure he hadn't missed any, he put them all in a line along the dry top of the pipe and counted them.

There were forty-two diamonds with their bluish shimmer. He had found them, and no one had seen him. He wrapped them in his handkerchief, put it in his pocket, took his tools off the wall and set off back.

Erika Waldis, a rather plump fifty-two-year-old from Weggis on the Rigi massif, was at the checkout of the Burgfelderstrasse shopping centre, entering the prices of the goods that the black conveyor belt was carrying along to the point where she could pick them up. Although it was very busy, her movements were slow and assured. She knew most of the prices off by heart. She picked up only vegetables, fruit, cheese and meat to read the cost before putting them in the trolley beside her. When the till had calculated the total, she said how much it was, waited for the customer to produce a banknote and gave them their change. Those were the few moments when she could stretch her back, look up and give the customers a smile. She knew most of the people by sight and was very popular, because she was always calm and did her best to keep the customers happy. She had time enough for that, eight and a half hours per day – that was how long she worked, there was no point in rushing things. After all, she was mainly dealing with food and one ought to take one's time over that, Erica thought.

Most of all she liked the slack times around nine in the morning and three in the afternoon. Then the shelves had a charm of their own, the air of an oasis of peace, where nothing bad could happen since there was plenty to eat, all healthy and nourishing. For example, there were twelve kinds of bread on offer, some made with soy flour, some with wheat bran and some with spelt. There were different kinds of yoghurt, plain and with fruit, with full-cream or skimmed milk. Recently there had even been organic potatoes, a bit more expensive than ordinary ones but still quite cheap. No one had to go hungry there.

Erika was at her most polite when she served the old women and men who did their shopping during the slack times. From the contents of their shopping trolleys she could tell which ones had only the state pension to live on and which had additional income. She would wait, with a friendly look on her face, until the old people had got out their purses, and watch patiently as they counted out the notes and coins to get as close as possible to the sum needed. They never handed over high-value notes; they didn't like parting with them.

She also liked serving the asylum seekers, the Tamils who lived in the block of flats next door. They were expensive modern flats but there was such a shortage of housing that the city had rented half of the block for asylum seekers. Erika knew that three or four of these slim brown men with pitch-black hair shared each room, twelve men in a three-room flat. Most couldn't understand a word of German, and Erika, who could only speak French along with German, because she'd spent a year looking after children in the Suisse Romande region, had great difficulty communicating with them.

It also sometimes happened that a woman who had just arrived from the Balkans or Anatolia would push her trolley, jam-packed with goods, to the checkout and expect to be able to pay with a twenty-franc note, since that was a lot of money in her home currency. Then Erika had to explain that in Switzerland twenty francs was not a lot, but was, in fact, a quite small amount of money, and it would only be enough for a small proportion of the goods in the trolley. But she was very careful in the way she did that so that none of them felt shown up.

That evening there was the usual lack of conversation at the checkout. The customers were waiting in lines some ten feet long. Men and women on their way home from work who wanted to make a quick purchase before the stores closed. Not unfriendly people but tired people, people who didn't have much time.

Since it was getting towards the end of the month and wages hadn't yet been paid, the trolleys mostly contained canned food, pasta and sausages, and very little fresh meat. It wasn't a wealthy district; the people who lived on Burgfelderstrasse were people like Erika herself: they had to count the pennies. She liked that, she felt at home.

When two foreign-looking men whom she immediately recognized as Turks reached the checkout, she said, "Güle güle," and gave them an almost familiar smile when they responded to her greeting – and wasn't in the least bothered by the looks of amazement from the other customers.

The police car drove into the Lohnhof car park. At the wheel was Sergeant Madörin, beside him Inspector Hunkeler; Corporal Lüdi, Kayat and the bald Swiss were squashed together in the back, the latter two handcuffed, and the rear doors were securely locked. There was no possibility of escape, even if one of them had thought of jumping out of the car while it was moving.

The blue light hadn't been switched on. There wouldn't have been much point in the rush-hour traffic anyway, and they had been instructed to attract as little attention as possible: since the protests by young people in the eighties, the police had not been exactly popular, so the more inconspicuous an operation was the better.

Very little had been said during the journey. Kayat had remained silent, as if the whole business had nothing to do with him. At first the bald man had protested loudly and gone on and on about it being a disgrace, a scandal, a police state. Since he was sitting by the door, he had at one point put all his strength into wrestling with the handle, trying to open it. But since no one in the car, not even Kayat, turned to look at him, he gave up and accepted his fate.

Hunkeler hated these silent journeys. He'd had two cigarettes, one after the other, which had annoyed him even as he lit them – he knew he couldn't stand this stupid smoking anymore, he was too old for it. He'd tried to give up several times but had never managed it, and now he felt he was too old to stop.

During the journey over Wettsteinbrücke into Greater Basel he looked across at the cathedral that rose up high over the Rhine. The roof was white with snow, shimmering in the darkness with an unreal brightness. When the car stopped outside the Lohnhof, he unlocked the rear doors, got out, and watched Kayat and the bald guy get out. Kayat put on a good show, like a true gentleman; the other had gone very pale – it was clear he was afraid. Madörin was standing beside them, like a watchdog on the alert. Hunkeler half expected him to bark.

All was quiet on the forecourt. The snowflakes were getting bigger and drifting down through the lamplight. St Leonhard's church with its late-Gothic filigree work was a stately presence behind the leafless lime trees. To the east were the gables of the Old Town.

Peter Hunkeler knew what was going to happen now. They would go into the office, they'd ask questions, the same ones again and again, both sides getting fed up with each other, and of course neither of the two would know anything about diamonds. If Kayat had actually had them on him, they'd be in the sewers by now. Anyone who fancied the idea could go and look for them. Hunkeler didn't fancy the idea at all.

"This way, gentlemen," he said, "this way, please." He went ahead through the door with a pointed arch that looked like the entrance to a monastery but which reminded him, however, of people sweating with fear, of cries and blows, of nervous breakdowns, and of those who had hanged themselves from the bars over the little windows. As he passed he waved to the porter bent over a crossword behind the window, his head on his hands, his elbows on his desk, and his eyes closed. Presumably he was asleep, but perhaps he was just reflecting on a word of five letters beginning with K, its third letter A.

They went through to the courtyard of the prison. The building with its two grey wings was over a hundred years old and permanently overcrowded with minor dealers and druggies who'd snatched old ladies' handbags to get money for their fix. There was a light shining behind one of the barred windows.

They went up some stairs and into Hunkeler's office. Lüdi took off their handcuffs and asked them to sit down. The bald guy demanded a lawyer, to which Lüdi responded with a nasty grin. "Take it easy," he said, "you'll get your lawyer soon enough."

Hunkeler went out into the corridor and got himself a cup of coffee. He sipped it as he stood there wondering whether he should have another cigarette. He was tired and found what was going on here so tedious he had to lean against the wall for a moment. He had the feeling he was falling, that he needed to lie down; he didn't want to see any more of this.

Suter, the public prosecutor, came out of one of the rooms further along. "Well," he said, "what's happened with the diamonds?"

Hunkeler shrugged.

"What's that supposed to mean?" Suter asked, as if he had no idea what that shrug might express.

"We haven't got them," Hunkeler said. "It's not my fault."

"We put five men on the operation," Suter said, with an indignant look, even though the business with the diamonds had nothing at all to do with him, "and you can't find anything? The German police give us reliable warning that a Beirut Connection courier with the proceeds of drug sales in the form of diamonds is on the Intercity from Frankfurt to Badischer Station, you're all there and yet you find nothing?"

Hunkeler took a sip of his coffee, which was still too hot. He knew very well that he had to let it all wash over him and he made an effort to look a bit guilty.

"And the courier?" Suter said, preparing for the final blow. "What about him? What was he called now?"

"Kayat," Hunkeler said. "He's in there with a Swiss guy whose identity has not yet been established."

"Well then," Suter said, working himself into a state, "start questioning the two of them finally, put the squeeze on them. We need results."

With that he turned away and swept off down the stairs.

Hunkeler dumped the still-hot cup of coffee in the plastic tub and went back into his office. Lüdi had gone out, but Schneeberger was still there examining the Lebanese man, who'd undressed down to his underpants. Madörin had put his black travel bag on the table and was taking one piece of underwear after another out of it. He shook each one, put it down on the table and stroked it, to see if there was anything hard sewn in. He then placed them one on top of the other, like a conscientious woman doing the ironing, grinning as he did so, as if he was enjoying himself.

Taking out the opened packet of condoms he grinned again and removed every French letter, counting them. "Nine," he said, "and where is the tenth?"

"I use a condom now and then," Kayat said apologetically. "I'm a careful man."

"On the train?" Madörin barked.

"That is a private matter," Kayat said. "It's nothing to do with you."

"The women seem to be after you all the time," Madörin said nastily, "with your looks."

"That's racist," Kayat countered coolly. "Just you watch what you say or I'll be making a complaint."

Madörin was close to boiling point, but he controlled himself, turned away and went over to Schneeberger. "Well?" he asked.

"Nothing," Schneeberger said, and, turning to Kayat: "You can get dressed again."

Lüdi came back in, planted himself in front of the bald man and said, "Your name is Anton Huber, date of birth 1938; you work as a chauffeur and you have a conviction for drunk driving."

"That was more than nine years ago," Huber said. "After ten years that sort of thing is deleted from your record. What has it to do with my being arrested here?"

"Why did you run over to this gentleman on the station concourse?" Lüdi asked, pointing at Kayat. "Why did you grab his arm?"

"I did what?" Huber said. "Can you prove it?"

31

"May I go now?" Kayat asked. "I have an appointment."

"Don't forget your French letters," Madörin said, "and be careful."

Hunkeler went over to the desk, stubbed out his cigarette in the ashtray and looked at the empty travel bag. There was something at the bottom that gleamed like dried snail slime. He put his hand in and ran the tip of his finger along it. It was clear that there had been something there that was now missing.

"Did you have the stones in there?" he said casually, as if he was asking about the weather.

"What on earth are you talking about?" Kayat said. "Can't you stop this nonsense? I've come to Switzerland as a perfectly ordinary tourist and I'd like to spend my time here as an ordinary tourist. Can't you see that?"

"Your name's in our computer," Hunkeler said. "It's true that you haven't any convictions but you've been a suspect for quite some time. You're suspected of being a courier – of drugs and the proceeds from drugs. We'd like to know on whose instructions you come and go so that we can catch them and take them to court, because we think we can't solve the drugs problem from below, from the street, but only from above, from the supply level. We want to arrest the people who earn millions from the addicts and take them to court. Do you understand that?"

Kayat had been listening with a look of interest. "Yes," he said, "I can understand that very well and I'm in complete agreement with you. But why are you telling me this?"

"You're just a filthy little courier," Hunkeler said, "a nasty rat who's shit-scared and flushes a million francs' worth of diamonds down into the sewers."

"That's slander," Kayat said, "racism and slander. What's the point of all this?"

"It's best if you clear off," Hunkeler said to Huber. "And you," he said, going up close to Kayat, "will stay here a while longer, take a laxative and shit everything out of your blasted bowels."

He turned and left.

Erika Waldis was on the traffic island waiting for a number 1 tram. It was snowing in large wet flakes, so she'd put her umbrella up. The snow floated through the light of the street lamp, settled on the asphalt and melted. Sheets, she thought, it's snowing sheets.

In her right hand she had her shopping bag with bread, milk and a smoked sausage. Even though she didn't have to pay cash in the branch where she worked but could buy things on credit and at a discount, she was careful not to buy too much, or anything too expensive, for she did have to pay eventually and money was tight.

For more than a year now she'd stopped lugging chocolate home by the kilo; she only ate it when things were bad. Then she would guzzle the brown blocks – with a guilty conscience, true, but with a strangely enjoyable sense of revenge – until she would slump on the sofa, exhausted, and fall into a short, dreamless sleep.

Now she was fine. She was looking forward to the thriller they were going to watch on Channel 2 after the news, she was looking forward to slipping into her warm bed.

When the green tram came, jingling, across the junction,

she got in. It wasn't a bad time to be going by tram, 7 p.m., the rush hour was over, the carriage half-empty. That was nice, she wouldn't have wanted to stand now, she was tired. At seven-thirty in the morning that didn't matter, she was still half-asleep then and hardly felt the bodies she had to squeeze through as she got on.

Erika took one of the single seats, leaned her umbrella against the wall so that it could drip dry, and put her bag on her lap. She watched as the tram set off. None of the other passengers were saying a word, they were all dozing. Despite that, Erika felt as if she were in a family. She wouldn't have wanted to be sitting alone in a car, driving from one red light to the next, she'd have felt lonely. She didn't have a driving licence anyway, and where would she keep a car? The parking bays in Lörracherstrasse, where she lived, were always taken.

She looked across at Kannenfeld Park, at the snow-covered trees, their branches bowed down to the ground. Some would break if the snow kept on like this.

The tram went down to Voltaplatz. At the crossroads were heavy long-distance trucks getting in each other's way. The tram had to wait several minutes before it could move on. It was like that every evening and every morning. Sometimes there was a truck from the food company she worked for, and then she tried to wave to the man at the wheel.

On Dreirosenbrücke, the tram was travelling almost silently along the rails. On the left-hand side were the tall, light-coloured buildings of the chemical factories. The windows were lit; the people there worked shifts.

Erika particularly liked travelling across the water. It was best of all in the morning in the summer months, when the sun was already up across the river. There at the bend in the

Rhein farther upstream you could see Mittlere Brücke, the two towers of the cathedral and, beyond them, the green hills of the Jura. That reminded you that Basel was a beautiful old town and you thought of holidays.

Now there was nothing to be seen. It was too dark and the snow obscured the view. Despite that, Erika wiped away the condensation on the window with her sleeve and put her forehead on the cold glass. Easter, she thought, at Easter she had a week's holiday and her intention was to go away with her lover Erdogan to Magliaso. She'd chosen that place on Lake Lugano because she'd been to a holiday camp there once with her youth group and even today she still thought it had been the most beautiful time of her life. It had been in the autumn, the woods were yellow and red and the chestnuts ripe, the church bells had rung every hour across the lake from Figino and for the whole two weeks there was nothing she'd had to do apart from a brief stint of washing-up each evening.

She'd suggested Magliaso to Erdogan when they'd been talking about going away for a week. And, for the first time since they'd been together, she'd insisted. At first he couldn't see why they should go away, he liked it here in Basel, he said, but she'd wanted to have him to herself for a few days. After all, here in Switzerland she was his wife and he her husband and that was that.

In April he'd have to go back to Turkey for three months anyway. He had to do that because he was a seasonal worker and they could spend at most nine months a year in Switzerland and were not allowed to bring anyone with them, neither wife nor children. Erika thought that was tough but in this particular case she had nothing against it.

Her plan was to make a diversion to visit her mother in Weggis on the way to the Canton of Ticino in the south. Erika was determined to do that, there was no question about it. She would introduce Erdogan to her mother as her fiancé with whom she was living even though they weren't yet married. And she would explain that marriage to a Turkish national, and him a Muslim, was very difficult. The main thing, of course, was that they were in love.

No one in Weggis needed to know that Erdogan had a wife and three children in Turkey. After all, Turkey was miles and miles away.

Erika thought she was happy. Not happy in the way the princesses and film stars that she read about in the women's magazines were, but a reliable happiness, the kind of happiness she'd always hoped for. If only things would stay as they were, that was her sole concern. And she would see to it that they did stay that way.

She got out at the first stop on the other side of the river, put up her umbrella and went down Breisacherstrasse to the house in Lörracherstrasse where she lived. It was an old red-brick building, like the others all round, that had been made available for the families of workers decades ago. Now it was somewhat dilapidated and the rent was cheap. It was mainly foreigners who lived there, so-called guest workers, some with their families, others with workmates. Not much Swiss German was spoken and there were Turkish and Italian stores on the street.

Erika opened the heavy wooden door to the passage that led into the courtyard. At the back was the joiner's workshop with its glass roof and stacks of planks. There was a smell of sawdust and at seven in the morning the screech of the bandsaw, hammering and sometimes the shouts of the workers could be heard.

The letterboxes on the left-hand wall of the passage were crammed full of brochures and free papers with almost nothing but adverts. They hadn't been cleared out for ages. No one there could read German and hardly anyone expected a letter. Some had fallen on the floor. Erika shook her head in disapproval. She would tidy it up on Sunday morning – on Sunday she had time. She opened her own letterbox, took everything out, locked it again, then went into the corridor on the left and up the stairs to her own apartment.

Erdogan wasn't home. She put her umbrella in the old butter churn she'd inherited from her grandmother, hung up her coat, had a quick look through the post and threw it in the trash can. Then she tapped the aquarium on the sideboard a few times to let the goldfish know she was back home. She sprinkled some food on the water and watched as the fish immediately swam up and started to eat. She put some water on to make peppermint tea, set the bread and smoked sausage on the low table by the settee, switched the TV on and started to eat.

By the time the thriller was getting towards the end Erika had fallen asleep. Still half in her dream she heard the front door open and the sound of steps. She opened her eyes. Erdogan was standing there in front of her, the snow on his hat and coat melting and dripping down off his sleeves. It didn't seem to bother him.

Erika sat up. She was about to start telling him off for all the drops of water and the imprint of his shoes on the fitted carpet. But then she saw that Erdogan was holding out a handkerchief. Lying on the handkerchief was a handful of diamonds. She realized at once what they were, even though she'd never seen such big diamonds in her life.

"Where did you get those?" she asked, suddenly wide awake.

"Found them," he whispered, "in the pipe."

"Whose are they?"

"No one saw me. They're mine."

Erika stood up, went over to the TV and switched it off. Then she grasped her thick blond hair, which she wore loose at home, and pulled it forward over her left shoulder. She went up to Erdogan, carefully took the handkerchief in both hands, sat down again and let the glittering stones roll round and round.

"Like little silver pebbles," she said quietly, "like shining drops of water." She put the handkerchief carefully down on the table and, pushing the sausage to one side, took the stones out one by one and placed them in a circle.

Erdogan, who had taken off his hat and coat and hung them up, came over slowly, almost shyly, and sat down beside her.

"No way you can keep them," Erika said after a while. "They must belong to someone."

"They belong to me," Erdogan insisted. "I'm a rich man now, not a shitty cleaner anymore, not an arsehole, not a bloody Turk. And you're a rich woman."

Putting her hair back again, Erika stood up, went over to the window and looked down into the yard before closing the curtains.

"Lock the front door," she said and then, after a short pause, "We've had a good life together until now, haven't we?"

*

Peter Hunkeler went down the steps to Barfüsserplatz. He was fed up and he needed a beer – and quickly. The smell of stale tobacco smoke and cold coffee in paper cups, the feverish know-it-all showing off, those fat arses in police trousers, those antiseptically clean corridors and those barred windows with despair dripping out of them and down the walls, covering them in mould – he couldn't stand it any longer. What did it mean he was? A destroyer of people, a well-drilled watchdog who locked them up, showing his teeth at every nod from above?

No, not at all. He was a sensitive lover of nature who liked nothing so much as his old cottage just across the border in Alsace, a man who knew about birds and could distinguish the call of the common redstart from that of the black redstart straight off. All the cats in the village would come running when they heard the sound of his car. They knew: it was good at Peter's place, at Peter's they were stroked, at Peter's they got meat out of tins.

Why then was he involved with this squad of simple-minded men, why had he let himself be appointed for life? "The police: your friend and helper" – he couldn't even raise a grin anymore at the stupid slogan some drunken copywriter had thought up. It was simply wrong. When in his long career had he ever been able to help a person in need, when had he ever appeared as a friend to any of the desperate figures there seemed to be more and more of every day in this town? In private, yes, there he would have been able to list a few whom he'd tried to pull out of the shit. But in his job? He couldn't think of any.

The job by which he earned his living consisted of tracking down, watching, arresting, convicting and locking up.

Taking in the petty drug dealers for a night behind bars, those pale, emaciated guys who were trying to finance their own fix by selling on a few grams of heroin, that was his job. He knew as well as his colleagues what hellish torment the junkies suffered when they were going cold turkey in prison. But that was the punishment for their addiction, as intended by the high-ups. Or harassing the hookers with faces like china that you could see from a long way off, if you were a policeman, that was his job, with the blessing of the high-ups.

That worthy policeman Corporal Lüdi, for example, was really determined to catch the druggies in flagrante. A few days ago Hunkeler had watched him ripping the needle out of the arm of a lad squatting on the ground. Did that kind of thing also have the blessing of the high-ups? And what kind of people were they at the top?

Certainly there were places on the street and elsewhere where they could get sterile needles in a heated room. But in the first place no one knew how long this arrangement would last after the recent political swing to the right and in the second they were not a long-term solution. The main problem, as Hunkeler had long known, was the criminalization of heroin. As long as heroin wasn't freely available at a sensible price, the wretchedness of the druggies would continue.

But why was heroin not freely available? The answer was clear: because there were powerful people who wanted to make money from heroin. And they could only make money when the stuff was banned. As soon as people could buy a fix from the local chemist's, just as you could buy a bottle of beer from the grocer's, the price would fall, for it was cheap to produce heroin.

But whenever you set about trying to identify the people behind the drug trafficking and drag them out into the light, the ones, that is, who earned money from the addicts by importing the forbidden stuff and using all sorts of crooked means to change it into clean, solid Swiss francs, you got nowhere. No one was guilty, no one knew anything, they all had clean hands. And if they suddenly tackled it with dogged determination, reactivating their long-dormant hunting instinct, they were called off by the high-ups. For they were men of honour, all of them, valuable pillars of society, members of boards of directors, old buddies of public prosecutors, friends since student days with members of parliament, and it was shameful and a stain on their honour for such worthy notables to be importuned.

Clearly this Kayat was a courier. The German police had issued precise details and they themselves had had their eye on him for a long time. But it was equally clear that they would have to let him go.

Serves him right, this Lebanese, Hunkeler thought as he went down the snow-covered steps, let him shit until he bursts, at least he'll have part of the punishment he deserves. He felt a malicious grin flit across his face, and he realized that he quite liked the man. He at least was in the front line, taking something of a risk, and that for relatively little money. He was a worthwhile opponent.

He went out onto Barfüsserplatz. Wet snow was running down the back of his neck; his hair must be dripping wet. The snow was now so thick that it had settled on the asphalt. The cars were going at walking pace, the pedestrians stepping carefully, some with pinched expressions, as if this snow was a great injustice, others half-amused. The

Barfüsserkirche across the square was as light and majestic as ever, the upper window and its gable slightly off to the left. Decades ago Hunkeler had wondered where this asymmetry came from, whether it was chance or planned and had some meaning. He'd asked art and history students about it but no one had an answer.

He went into the Rio Bar, had a good look round, then joined Ralf, who was sitting at a table by the window on the right reading a newspaper. Ralf was the sports editor for the only serious local paper. They'd got to know each other when they'd both done the initial semesters of law. They'd sat there, bored, in lecture theatre 16, surrounded by keen students, the two of them staring out of the high windows at the elms and lime trees on Petersplatz; after the lectures they used to go for a beer in the Harmonie and talk about the things that really interested them. Back then Hunkeler had been a fan of Georges Brassens and *Porte des Lilas*, while Ralf had just discovered Jacques Brel. Once or twice after an evening's pub crawl they'd taken the night train to Paris and reappeared in the lecture theatre a few days later, dishevelled and exhausted but feeling immensely superior to their fellow students.

Ralf had then dropped out and gone to work for the newspaper. He had started off as a theatre critic, writing reviews that were arrogant and unusually caustic. They made him well known but caused the editor, who was a friend of the manager, to move him over to sport.

At the time, Hunkeler, having inherited some money from a mentally deficient uncle who'd died young, had gone to Paris to be a *clochard*, as he had revealed at the window table in the Rio Bar. He'd lived in the Latin Quarter, in a garret with no heating; he couldn't even stand up straight, but he'd felt really good there, better than he'd ever felt in his whole life. He'd actually made contact with a few *clochards* who slept on the grille over the air vent of the Métro by the Relais de l'Odéon. He'd spent the night there himself a few times, lying alongside the old, hunched-up figures, but then he'd gone back to his garret. He wasn't a *clochard*, he'd no reason to be one.

He could easily have stayed on in Paris, he liked the life there very much. But then he went back to Basel after all to continue his studies.

Perhaps it was all down to chance. It was chance that soon after that he met his future wife, from whom he was now divorced. It was pure chance that he'd given up his studies and joined the Basel police after his first child was born. And it was chance that now, on that day and at that time, he was sitting in this bar.

At first sight the Rio Bar had changed little since those days. There were still wide mirrors on the wall, as in a French bistro, and the tables were still separated by wooden partitions. Even the clientele appeared to have remained the same for decades: students of both sexes, women painters, boozy bachelors and the occasional grass widower. The noise level was as high as ever and the air was thick enough to cut, but the openness had gone, the positive sense that things were about to change.

It was joy that was lacking. That was what struck Hunkeler. There was no hearty laughter. No one seemed to enjoy being able to sit there drinking wine or coffee, no one seemed determined to paint the town red again, nowhere was there the slightest hint of lust, of eroticism, and the manager, sitting at her desk, pale and blond, looked like a lifeless doll. Just a load of stale shit, Hunkeler thought, a crowd of affluent idiots, a collection of feeble-minded bores, all the ambience of a nice, conformist barber's.

Hunkeler didn't feel there was anyone he'd like to talk to, he didn't want to get involved with any of them at all, not at any of the tables or even at the bar. He felt as out-of-place as a farmer in a beauty salon, and he wondered whether the lousy mood he felt all around wasn't perhaps something he was projecting out into the room himself. What kind of person was he anyway, he wondered. Would he still be able to enjoy a rave-up? Did he even want to anymore? No, that was all over, there were professional reasons why he couldn't do that in public these days. Wasn't he nothing more than a tart living off the affluent society? That's what he was, no doubt about it: a state official who'd sold out for a decent salary, a Christmas bonus and a substantial pension.

He picked up the glass of beer the Tamil waiter had brought, lifted it to his lips and emptied it in lovely, slow, regular swigs. "Right then," he said out loud as he put his glass down, "there's no point in all this."

Ralf lowered his newspaper. "Aren't you feeling well?" he asked.

"No," Hunkeler said, "no bastard can stand this."

"Ignore it," Ralf said, taking up his newspaper again, "get plastered and have a good sleep."

Hunkeler leaned back, closed his eyes and wrapped himself up in memories. His young days, he thought, days of promise, of offers, of boundless trust. Your hand on the knee of the girl beside you, her eyes shining. Or a strand of blond hair across a freckled face. Wide eyes that want to love. A cheek leaning on your shoulder. A girl's tongue briefly forcing itself between your lips. Then going home across the dark, empty town, walking in step without a word, your hand on her right hip, feeling it sway. Quietly opening the front door, climbing the stairs, taking care not to make them creak too loudly. Going into the garret, a brief giggle. Then running your hand through her hair and tumbling into bed with her in a tangle of curiosity.

After his third beer Hunkeler got up from his chair at the table by the window, pushed his way through the people at the bar and went into the toilet. His hand against the tiled wall to steady himself, he peed and thought. Afterwards he put some coppers in the telephone in the little vestibule and dialled. It was Schneeberger who answered.

"And?" Hunkeler asked.

"Nothing," Schneeberger said. "His bowels are empty, there's nothing in them anymore."

"Let him go," Hunkeler said, "but keep an eye on him. Around the clock. And on Huber as well."

"Of course," Schneeberger said, hanging up.

Hunkeler left the bar and hailed a taxi on Barfüsserplatz. He could have taken a tram home, but he wanted things to be different that evening. He wanted to live it up a bit.

The car drove slowly through the falling snow. Like a ship, Hunkeler thought, a soft silent boat. Or like the snowplough when he was a child out in the country and four horses dragged the triangular contraption made of heavy beams through the knee-deep snow. He remembered Fridolin, the farmhand who looked after the horses, sitting at the front, pipe in mouth, inviting him to join him up there.

In this way they'd gone round the area where he lived, all glorious in the snow.

He got out of the taxi by the Sommereck, a restaurant not far from his house, and went in. The manager, Edi, a former sailor who'd worked as a cook on a steamer in the Caribbean, was sitting at the regulars' table, along with Walti, a guitar teacher, who had constant trouble with his gall bladder, and Beat, who sold second-hand furniture, mostly from houses that were being cleared.

Hunkeler joined them. He felt at ease there, he could relax at this table better than he could anywhere else: the well-scrubbed beechwood table, the oil stove with its long black pipe, the clock on the wall striking the hour with its deep note – all that had a solid, comforting reality. And the conversations were the same, measured with long pauses. When one of them was speaking, the others listened. No one would have dreamed of interrupting; they were all allowed to say what they had to say. There was music from the jukebox that Edi had brought back from the Caribbean, songs in English and Spanish with many verses, sung by singers who had never become widely known, simple, beautiful poetry, "Working for the Yankee dollar, yeah".

Erika Waldis was lying in bed, hands behind her head. She could hear the circular saw from the carpenter's in the yard that had been switched on a few minutes before, she could hear Erdogan's regular snore. One of his legs was across her thighs and he'd put his right arm across her breast. Like a little monkey, she thought, clinging on to its mother.

She hadn't slept well that night, she'd kept waking up, thinking about the diamonds that were on the coffee table. She didn't like those stones at all. A few times she'd thought of throwing them down the lavatory and flushing them away. But she knew that would lead to a huge row, and she liked rows even less.

She'd decided to accept her fate, she had no other choice. The diamonds were there and Erdogan would never give them up of his own free will, that much was clear. It was just as clear to her that, like it or not, those glittering stones with their glint of blue were going to rule her life in the days to come. For of course Erdogan wouldn't simply store them away somewhere; he'd want to sell them, to turn them into ready cash. And he wouldn't simply pay the money into a bank, he'd invest it, possibly even in Turkey – and she knew what that meant.

Erika was determined to do everything to keep Erdogan. She realized that he wouldn't stay with her for ever, but she wanted him to stay as long as possible. She'd had enough of being without a man, of the empty double bed, of sitting watching TV by herself. She wanted to have a man beside her, one who was kind to her, who liked her, who listened to her when she had something to say. One beside whom she could go to sleep and wake up the next morning.

Sex meant nothing to her – she couldn't care less about it. Erdogan wanted it now and again, and with amiable reserve she always allowed him to have it. She didn't enjoy the sex as such, it felt quite alien to her. But what she did like was Erdogan's exhaustion after it, the way he immediately fell asleep, breathing deeply. Without it she'd have had no idea what was the point of her full breasts, her genital organs. She had no children and she was happy with that.

Apart from Erdogan she only had her mother and Nelly, who also worked in the supermarket. Her mother was over eighty now and all she got when she went to see her was grumbling and groaning. And since she'd been living with Erdogan her relationship with Nelly had cooled as well.

The two women had planned a fortnight's walking holiday on a Greek island, but Erika had cried off at short notice because of the trip to Magliaso, which had clearly hurt Nelly's feelings. Or at least she'd heard nothing from her since then. Having a woman friend was all well and good, Erika thought, a woman friend could help you when you needed it and you could rely on her. A woman friend was someone you had all your life, with the occasional break, perhaps.

It just so happened that a man was more important.

Erika couldn't really say why that was the case. She'd never thought about it very much, she'd never been bothered about that kind of thing. It was just the way things were. She wasn't the one who'd set up the world, she'd just found herself in a world where certain rules operated and she'd learned to stick to those rules. It was best like that. And, as everyone knew, a life without a man was only a halfway house. Say what you like, that was the way things were. And she'd been lucky with Erdogan. He treated her decently, he was kind and considerate to her. There was a delicacy about him she'd never come across anywhere else. It was something oriental, something that reminded her of the frankincense and myrrh she'd heard about in religious education lessons at school. She'd never seen a real mosque but as a child she'd had a book of fairy tales with stories about Aladdin and his magic lamp, Ali Baba, Sinbad the Sailor and Scheherazade with her slender limbs and black eyes. There was a picture of a fairy-tale town on the title page with a dozen minarets rising up against a dark-blue sky with a golden half-moon. She knew the town was called Istanbul, the city on the Bosphorus, on the Golden Horn, the city of Sultan Suleiman the Magnificent with his seraglio.

She would have loved to go there, when she was young, before all this travelling around had become so popular. She'd never managed it, however, like so many other things, probably because she'd never really tried – the real Istanbul couldn't be as beautiful as the one on the title page.

Even now she'd have liked to go there, with Erdogan; and to Ephesus as well, which was near his home. She knew she'd never do that. In his own country, in the environment where he belonged, he would disappear. She would lose him at once.

Her love for Erdogan was only possible outside Turkey. The best place for it was here in Switzerland, in Basel, in this apartment.

When the alarm clock sounded, Erika switched it off. She got up, went into the kitchen, put some water on and set the coffee table in the living room. The diamonds she left there, in a circle; she didn't dare disarrange them.

When she brought the coffee in, Erdogan was awake. "I'm not going to work today," he said, "and you're not either."

She'd expected something like that. She didn't respond immediately, for she had to think it over first and that took time early in the morning just after she'd got up. She poured herself a coffee, added milk, had a drink, then took a piece of chocolate out of the box and said, "That would be the most stupid thing we could do, people would notice."

Erdogan sat up but didn't get out of bed; he sat on the edge, rubbing his teeth and yawning. "Call Nelly and get her to stand in for you. And I've got toothache so I can't go to work. We're skipping work today. We're celebrating today. I'm rich today."

And she knew she couldn't argue.

Guy Kayat had a hard night behind him. Lying in his bed in the Drei Könige Hotel, he could hear the horn of a barge out on the Rhine. His bed seemed to be shaking from the thump-thump of the boat's engine, but that was presumably just his imagination. Kayat could feel himself shivering. He'd had to get up several times in the night to go to the lavatory and between them he'd fallen into a light, nervous sleep. They'd really fucked him up in the Lohnhof, those arse-lickers, he thought, but then he'd fucked them over as well. They hadn't found the diamonds and they'd no proof against him.

He got up and went over to the window. Outside the Rhine was flowing past in the early light of dawn. Right underneath the window a man in a yellow anorak and smoking a pipe was on the towpath, fishing. It was still snowing, the houses across the water were behind a curtain of snowflakes. The barge was having difficulty progressing, the horn sounded once more, a dull, drawn-out sound. There was a light in the wheelhouse above the captain's cabin. At the wheel was a man, unmoving, his eyes fixed upriver, on the arch of Mittlere Brücke that he was aiming for.

Kayat went over to the phone, picked up the receiver and ordered salmon for breakfast. Then he sat down at the table and thought.

He was being kept under observation, that much was clear. Presumably the best thing to do was to stay quietly in his room and look after himself. Something had gone wrong. He'd no idea what it was but he wasn't to blame. The priority was to keep the channels secret, that was essential for his work. He estimated that the diamonds must have been worth something like a million dollars. That was a lot of money, but for the Connection it was chicken feed. The decisive fact was that the stones hadn't fallen into the hands of the police. They would have been evidence, a clear fact that couldn't be denied. There would have been no plausible explanation for their presence. Of course it wasn't forbidden to take diamonds across the border, but how could he be expected to explain how he came to be in possession of such an immensely valuable quantity?

It was his job to answer all the questions with silence, and naturally he had kept his mouth shut. He wasn't tired of life. They could have kept him on remand in prison for weeks or months on end.

Kayat was certain that the people for whom the diamonds were destined wouldn't have lifted a finger to help him. They expected him to be silent as the grave. And they had the right to leave him to his fate should something go wrong. That was the risk he was taking.

If the police had found them, the diamonds would have been lost anyway. They were too dirty. And presumably, had the police found them, they would have been confiscated as proceeds from drugs and used for the campaign against drugs. And that would not have been what the Connection intended.

Of the source of the leak that had betrayed him, Kayat had no idea. Nor did he waste his time worrying about it. Who was he? Nothing but a minor dogsbody for the drugs criminals, nothing but a little courier. One of the main requirements of his work was that he should know nothing. He knew neither who had sent nor who was to receive the consignment – that would have been far too risky. What he did know was that a bald Swiss with the code name of Gustav would be waiting for him at Badischer Station. He had also memorized a secret phone number he could dial in case of emergency, but only with the greatest precaution. He hadn't written it down, he'd stored it inside his head: 123 63 20.

The leak must be somewhere right at the top, Kayat thought, as he poured himself a cup of the tea the waiter had brought. He had already had his suspicions when the customs official had scrutinized him so conspicuously. But that could have been mere chance. That the police had been waiting for him at the station was clear. They'd had a whole squad ready there and he'd only escaped for a brief but decisive moment thanks to the family with the child.

Someone had warned the Basel police and given them precise information. And they hadn't arrested him as he got off the train but had waited until he met the bald man. Why had they done that? Because they didn't want him, the little courier, but the man who received the goods. He would have led them to those behind the operation, that's what it was all about.

His situation, Kayat thought, picking up a slice of salmon with the fork and adding a few capers, was anything but pleasant. Not just that the police were after him, he was used to that by now. At least as unpleasant was the fact that he had been betrayed. For that meant that some high-up in the drugs business was trying to put Kayat's boss out of action. It also meant that some powerful drugs bosses were at war – a war between two cartels. And that war was threatening to destroy him, the little courier.

Kayat had had enough. He should have got out ages ago, certainly before this trip to Basel. So far everything had gone perfectly, he'd been well paid and had saved enough to buy a hotel in Cyprus. But anyone who's got a bit of money always wants a bit more, and anyone who's got a bit more wants a bit more still. It was a spiral. He'd long been aware of that, but had been convinced he could give up at the right moment.

Now, however, there was no thought of an elegant farewell. He didn't just have to shake off the police, he also had to make contact with the man for whom the diamonds were intended, he had to explain what had happened. He had to convince the people he'd behaved honestly, otherwise his life would soon be over.

The main difficulty would be to establish contact without the police noticing.

He couldn't rely on that Huber, he was no use. Strange, Kayat thought, as he poured himself more tea, that idiots were used as intermediaries in this very successful country. A cretin like that would never have survived in Beirut or Nicosia, he'd have long since been eaten by the wolves.

After he'd finished breakfast, he lay back down on

the bed and pulled the blanket up over his ears. He was exhausted but he could feel that his stomach had calmed down. Wait and see, he thought, wait and see what happens.

When Peter Hunkeler woke, he was in the bed of his lover Hedwig, a divorcee. He realized that even before he opened his eyes. He heard the regular snores that rose to a high whistling note as she breathed in, he smelt the familiar woman's smell, and felt the warm thighs that lay against his legs.

In the faint light of the street lamp reflected from the ceiling he contemplated the plump woman's body beside him: apart from the reddish skin on the back of her neck, half-covered by her light straggly hair, the sweaty skin over the outline of her spine and the rolls of fat on either side were snow-white.

She'd been sleeping in his arms, her back against his belly. She loved that and he loved it too.

He turned his head to look at the alarm clock. It was shortly after seven. There wasn't much traffic to be heard outside. The blessed calm of the morning, Hunkeler thought, the tender hour of lovers. Placing a kiss on Hedwig's shoulder, he drew his right leg out from under her hip. He knew that she would stop snoring for a moment and he was satisfied to see that that was exactly what happened. Anyone who knows the snoring habits of a person, Hunkeler thought, isn't alone, and then said softly: Old goat that I am.

He almost had to laugh but his headache prevented it. That Edi with his grappa, that regulars' table in the

Sommereck with its Caribbean music, "Working for the Yankee dollar, yeah", that delicate male friendship until the early hours, and he'd ended up in Hedwig's double bed, of course, even though he hadn't arranged to come. But that was just the way things were. You told yourself you'd had enough of women, you'd never lie down between two fat thighs again, because sooner or later it was going to end in a war you had no stomach for, since you were one of the marriage-wounded, a *mutilé de la guerre de mariage*, and then, after all, you found yourself on top of a woman again. The double beds remained, the partners changed. And it was right that way, Hunkeler thought, you should share beds but not apartments.

He got up, went into the kitchen, put on some water for tea and coffee. Coffee for Hedwig, tea for himself. Coffee and tea went very well together.

He found Hedwig awe-inspiring. She could give her love freely and extravagantly because she was happy with herself: her heart remained her own and that heart radiated a warm light that was enchanting. What's more, she could go out walking in her body – which definitely wasn't the kind you saw in adverts nowadays: those skinny cows with a stupid smile on their faces – with a relaxed grandeur and, when she felt like it, could advertise it with a charming warmth that said: Anyone who wants me can have me, if the situation is right. But none of those randy goats should imagine they can move in with me, they're all just too stupid.

That was the way Hunkeler saw things as he stood by the stove watching the first bubbles rise from the bottom of the pan. That night she'd behaved like a real lady again. He'd rung the bell of the high-rise in the street that ran past

Kannenfeld Park simply because he didn't want to spend the night in his own empty apartment. She'd had a quick look down out of the seventh-floor window, then pressed the button for the door. He'd gone up in the lift and when he went into her apartment, she was already back in bed. He'd crawled in to join her, she'd immediately sat up on top of him, set about moving her heavy bottom and when it was over they'd gone to sleep.

Once the smell of coffee was floating round the apartment she came to the little table in the kitchen that he'd set. "How's things?" she asked.

"Better," Hunkeler said, pouring himself some tea.

"You're in the wrong job. Running around after these young guys who need drugs, that's not for you. And you get pretty drunk now and then as well."

"That was the grappa," Hunkeler said, "that was one of Edi's scandalous grappa ambushes."

"You men," Hedwig said, "you men are always wanting to get drunk. At least, men I like. Why should that be?"

"I didn't get really drunk," Hunkeler objected, "though I definitely would have if I hadn't known I could sleep in your bed."

"It's good that you're here." She cut off a slice of cheese. She sat there like a walrus, agreeably assured and with a bright charm, despite still being half-asleep – like one of Picasso's bulky pink women, Hunkeler thought.

"It's OK for you," she said. "You can go back to bed and sleep for another half-hour, while I have to go to school and deal with the children."

"Wrong, it's you who's OK, you've got bright young things waiting for you. There's only arseholes waiting for me."

"Two weeks ago they closed Platzspitz Park in Zurich, the one people had started calling 'needle park'. Where are the druggies to go now? They can't go to a bar and order a half of heroin. I just don't understand it." She put butter on her bread and spread some runny honey over it. "Everyone knows that there are drug addicts and that those addicts urgently need their drugs and will do anything to get them. Despite that, they take them away from them."

"Wrong again," Hunkeler objected. "They don't take them away from them, they just make them dearer."

He got up and went into the bathroom for a shower. The warm water ran down his chest and over his bulging belly. It calmed him down. What did he actually have to do with drugs? What did he care about Platzspitz Park and that stupid, disgraceful campaign against the druggies? He wanted to wallow in warm water, that was all he wanted. Like a hippo, like a crocodile together with a rosy-pink walrus.

He left Hedwig's apartment just before nine and took the tram to the Lohnhof. Schneeberger and Madörin were already in the office, mercilessly setting a good example. Suter, the state prosecutor, had the telephone in his hand – and he was speaking standard German, not Swiss German, in a clear, firm, officer's voice. Clearly it was the German police on the other end of the line.

"I don't know how that could have happened," Suter said. "The guy must have suspected something, he ran off to the toilet incredibly quickly. Yes, the men's toilet. Exactly. I presume they're somewhere in the sewers now. Or they're on their way down the Rhine to you, hahaha." His laughter sounded rather forced. "Yes, that's right, it was something of a flop. But I ask you, that kind of thing can happen to the German police as well, it goes with the job. As you say, just as you say, my friend. We don't have to put up with criticism like that. Goodbye."

He put the receiver down and gave Hunkeler an angry look. "Now the fat's in the fire," he said. "They're complaining to me, even though I've had as good as nothing to do with the business. The next time they'll be wondering whether it's worth giving us a tip-off." He frowned nastily. "The way you look, Inspector. Have you had one too many again? And you think you can catch the drug smugglers. You're useless, completely useless." He went to the door, yanked it open and bounced out, slamming the door behind him. Then there was silence.

Hunkeler lit a cigarette, it was the first of the morning and it didn't taste good.

"Right then," Schneeberger said, after a pause during which he seemed to have been waiting for something, "so let's get on with it. In the first place, as I told you on the telephone yesterday – to go by the noise you were calling from the Rio Bar?"

"Exactly," Hunkeler said.

"We couldn't prove anything against that Kayat, nothing at all. A heavy guy." "Heavy" had recently become Schneeberger's favourite expression, used to denote great respect. "Nothing on his body, nothing inside, really clean. He's staying at the Drei Könige, as is right for a businessman of his standing. Anton Huber, with a record, lives at 34 Gempenfluhstrasse, ground floor, in a house that belongs to the Infex Corporation, import–export. And Infex, for its part, belongs to Herr Dr Zeugin, former fiduciary agent and for many years a prominent member of the Basel Cantonal Parliament."

Schneeberger fell silent, his right hand heavy on the table.

Hunkeler could feel his neck stiffening. "Zeugin, that patron of the arts who wants to get into the national parliament in the autumn?"

"The very man," Schneeberger said. "He's also president of the Culture for Basel society, the next project of those culture-vultures being 'The World in Song'."

Hunkeler fished another cigarette out of the packet. Over the flame of the match he looked out at the bare maple tree in the yard outside. Three crows were perched on one branch, black, powerful birds with shimmering plumage.

"That's just a coincidence," he said after he'd put the match out. He took a deep drag on his cigarette and at once felt better. "Huber has to live somewhere or other." He paused to blow out the smoke. "What does this Infex deal in?"

"Tobacco, toiletries and so on. They own several trucks, which are used for international transport. They're sealed and can't be opened when they cross borders as long as the papers are in order."

"I know," said Hunkeler, "that's to expedite customs clearance."

"Then you'll also know," Schneeberger went on like a dachshund on the scent, "that these TIR trucks are sometimes used for smuggling goods, sometimes, so I've heard, with the tacit connivance of senior officials."

"It's said that drugs are also smuggled in those trucks," Madörin interjected, as if the business had nothing to do with him.

"So you think," Hunkeler said after a pause which he'd spent scrutinizing the table top – it was hard, fine-grained beechwood – on which Schneeberger's right hand was resting, "you think this Zeugin is involved in drug trafficking, and on a large scale, Huber being the contact with Kayat and the diamonds intended for Infex?"

"What makes you think that?" Schneeberger asked, not turning a hair.

"They're stories out of the *Arabian Nights*," Hunkeler said, "if you know what I mean."

Schneeberger slowly shook his head. "I've never read those fairy tales. I only read the newspaper. And there it says that the worldwide annual turnover in drugs is estimated at over five hundred million dollars."

"What I meant," Hunkeler went on, "is that there are no diamonds to be seen anywhere at all and that we won't get any further as long as it stays that way."

At this Madörin joined in again. "I presume that means we absolutely have to find those diamonds. And if Kayat really did flush them down the toilet, someone will just have to go down there to take a look. Only who wants to do something like that?"

"In the first place," Hunkeler said, "you might just as well go looking for the proverbial needle in a haystack as diamonds in the sewers. If they ever were down there, they won't be down there any longer, they'll have been flushed out into the treatment plant – and you just try to find a handful of diamonds in the treatment plant. In the second place, and this second point seems to contradict the first, which is not quite the case, however: if this Kayat really did flush the diamonds away, he'll have to justify his action to whoever he's working for. So we still have the possibility of finding this guy. In all probability he'll give Kayat hell, and that will make him do everything he can to try and find the diamonds again. Wherever he looks, we must be there as well. So we have to let ourselves be guided by him. If we start rummaging round in the sewers right away, he may well notice and disappear for good. That means that for the moment we can do nothing but sit here quietly and wait."

"Or get drunk," Schneeberger said nastily.

"I'm the one who gives the orders here," Hunkeler said calmly, "and I'm the one who decides in the bar what and how much I'm going to drink. Anything else?"

"Yes," Madörin said, "should we keep an eye on Zeugin as well?"

"No," Hunkeler said. Then, after a while, "I'll see to him myself."

Around eleven on that same day Erika and Erdogan were walking along Freie Strasse. She'd linked arms with him, even though he didn't like it. Only whores do that, he'd said when she'd tried it for the first time, but she'd refused to give in. She wanted to have a man with whom she could go down the street arm in arm, and that was that.

It was a normal workday, a Tuesday morning like any other Tuesday morning, except that it had been snowing the whole night through. The snow had been cleared from the road and both pavements but so much was falling that it kept building up and it was three feet high along the gutters. The people who were out shopping and on errands had their collars up. Some were visibly disgruntled at the lousy weather and forced their way ahead, without looking whether anyone was coming the other way.

That didn't bother Erika. She wasn't at all in a hurry. She even liked the fact that it was snowing, it reminded her of her young days on the Rigi. And she had something she had long wished for: a free workday she could spend in town with Erdogan, for he did a five-day week, and on Saturdays, when he was free, she was sitting at the checkout.

Standing looking at the window display with the gold rings and incredibly expensive, glittering stones, the pair of them became nervous for a moment. She could feel Erdogan pulling at her arm and she almost gave way. But she stood firm and said, "No way. We're here now and we're going in."

They went into the store, then stood there, still arm in arm, until Erdogan closed the umbrella and put it in the stand in the corner.

A young woman came out of one of the rooms at the back. "Yes," she said, "can I help you?"

"Certainly," Erika said, determined to go ahead. "You see, we've got two diamonds and we'd like to know how much they're worth."

She went up to the glass-topped counter; there were all sorts of jewellery on display under it, but she ignored that. Opening her handbag she took out a handkerchief embroidered with roses, unfolded it and placed it on the glass. On it were two diamonds sparkling with a bluish light.

The young woman picked up one of the stones, put something like a magnifying glass over her left eye and checked them meticulously without a word. "Where did you get them?" she asked after a while, still concentrating on the stone.

"Inherited," Erika said, "inherited from my grandmother."

"Oh really?"

Alarmed all of a sudden, Erika swallowed and said, "We've changed our mind. Give them back to me, please." She held out her hand.

"One moment," the woman said. "Please take a seat." And she disappeared into the back of the store.

Erika looked round. On the right were two chairs. She took Erdogan by the arm and they both sat down. Without exchanging a word they waited until the young woman reappeared. With her was an oldish man with bushy white eyebrows. Holding the diamond between thumb and forefinger of his left hand, he shut his left eye, looked the stone over with his other and said, "I'll give you 5,000 francs for a diamond like that."

Erika stood up. "We're sorry," she said, "but we've decided not to sell them. Please give it back to me."

"You said it was inherited," the jeweller went on, "from your grandmother. Is that the case?"

"That's none of your business," Erdogan said. "Give us back the diamond or I'll call the police."

"Really," the jeweller said, "you're going to call the police? Go ahead then."

His eyes still fixed on the diamond, he said after a while, "For the two diamonds I'll give you 12,000 francs."

Carefully replacing the diamond on the handkerchief, he looked up. He had grey, expressionless eyes. "May I ask if you're Turkish?" he said. "And if that is indeed the case, which I do not doubt, I would like to ask you how you came into possession of these two diamonds." He was almost smiling, and the expression in his eyes seemed suddenly inviting.

"This man's nationality is no business of yours," Erika said firmly. "Who do you think you are, the Shah of Persia perhaps?"

She picked up the handkerchief with the two stones, put it in her pocket and went out, pulling Erdogan with her.

They quickly walked up Freie Strasse, turned into an alleyway on the left near the top and only stopped when they were by the red-sandstone facade of the cathedral.

"Put the umbrella up," she said, "we're getting quite wet and people are looking at us."

Erdogan put the umbrella up and held it carefully over her head. He didn't seem to know what to do and kept on looking apprehensively back up the alleyway. "There's no one following us," Erika said, "and he doesn't know our names. Let's just behave as if we're tourists. Look," she said, pointing to a figure on horseback over the left-hand entrance that was stabbing a little dragon with his lance, "that's St George. He killed the dragon."

They went into the cathedral, still arm in arm, walked down the left-hand aisle and sat in a pew at the bottom. In front of them was the stone relief with the four stations showing how St Vincent was tortured and burned on a red-hot gridiron and then rose again from the dead. Erika liked that very much, it was like something from a book of fairy tales and she almost forgot about the jeweller.

"If he'll pay 6,000 francs for one diamond," Erdogan said, "then that makes over 200,000 francs for all of them together. With that I could have a little hotel built on the coast outside Selçuk. I mean, with those 200,000 francs in my hand the bank would give me credit for a new hotel."

"No," Erika said, "we're not selling them. You saw the way he was immediately suspicious. And if he reports it to the police they'll arrest you for not handing in lost property. That's the law."

"I'll sell them in another store," Erdogan said, "where they're not suspicious. Then I'll buy a car. I've got a driving licence."

"That's not a good idea. You have to continue living as you always have. Otherwise people will notice and wonder where you got the money for the car."

Erdogan thought for a while. Then he said, "No. I'm wealthy. And I want to enjoy my wealth. Everyone has a car, that's not something people notice."

"The diamonds aren't going to be sold. If you like I'll take out a personal loan. You can buy a car with that and we'll tell people I took out a loan."

"If you like," Erdogan said, "that's what we'll do."

Three hours later Erdogan was at the wheel of an old, white American car with a red sliding roof that the driver could open by pressing a button. The interior – the partly torn leather seats, the dashboard and the steering wheel – was red as well. Erika had thought it was somewhat extravagant when they'd examined it at the used-car market, but Erdogan had immediately decided it was the old crock he wanted to buy. They'd paid for it with the personal loan she'd taken out in the town centre shortly before, and then, having dealt with the paperwork, they drove away.

Erdogan had driven the car in the midday traffic, quickly getting accustomed to the gear change. It was clear that he'd often been at the wheel of a car. Erika wondered when that could have been, back in Turkey or even in Switzerland, but she didn't ask him. That was one of the rules they both stuck to – no questions about their previous lives. The snow was falling incessantly, the air full of flakes, but the windshield wipers kept going. The car made a good impression on her. It was solidly built and didn't threaten to fall apart at any moment. The seats were comfortable as well. It was a luxury car Erdogan was driving and with the roof open in the summer it would be a real limousine.

They hadn't said a word to each other since they set off from the used-car market. They were enjoying going for a drive together, sitting beside each other as they drove safely through the snow. At first they'd been nervous, tense about the adventure that lay ahead of them, about the freedom of being able to take any road, any side street, in any direction.

Erika had noticed how calm Erdogan had become, assured and deliberate, like a fisherman going out to sea in his boat, and she'd leaned back in her seat, relaxed and at ease. After all, they had a free afternoon to look forward to.

"The Gempenfluh," she said, "we'll drive out to the Gempenfluh."

"The Gempenfluh? Where's that?"

"It's a hill with a viewpoint," Erika said. "It's in the Jura, just south of the town. There's an inn up there."

"That's good," Erdogan said, "I'm starting to get hungry."

He put his arm round her shoulder, drawing her to him and laughing his deep, heartfelt laugh. Then he started to sing, a Turkish song she couldn't understand a word of. When he realized he began to whistle instead, repeating the same tune a dozen times over, as if he were telling a story in several verses.

The snow at the side of the road was two feet high. It was weighing down the young beech trees so that they were almost touching the red soft top.

"Have we got winter tyres on?" she asked.

"Not necessary," Erdogan said, "it's OK even with summer tyres."

She looked at his brown, sinewy fingers on the steering wheel; they seemed beautiful to her. She knew he was from a family of small farmers. His father, his grandfather and his great-grandfather had all been farmers, he told her, all in the same village, the same house, not far from Selçuk, on the edge of the river delta.

Erdogan had mentioned the name of the village he came from, but he had said it so quickly and indistinctly that she couldn't remember it. All that she knew was that in the spring the storks returned and built their nests on the roofs and caught frogs on the delta. The day when the first stork appeared was a holiday, with everyone celebrating through the night because it meant the end of winter. And in the evenings the flamingos from the swamps would gather in one large flock and fly across the sky making it dark below. The way he described it, it was clear it was a beautiful sight.

It was a relatively young farmer's son sitting next to her and she liked that, for she was a farmer's daughter, if not all that young anymore, but you never lost your farming background. They had to stick together, Erdogan and her, she'd known that from the very first when she noticed him at the checkout. They were from the same class, if not from the same country. But class was more important; you could ignore the country. On the steering wheel were the two beautiful hands of a small-time farmer and Erika trusted those hands.

The car was running smoothly between the snow-covered trees, slowly and steadily. A couple of times the drive wheels threatened to skid and the car was close to going out of control, but then the tyres gripped the road surface again and the car stayed on track. But there was ice on the big bend at the top, before the road left the forest, and the car couldn't manage that. It slid to the side, and the more Erdogan put his foot down, the more the vehicle was heading for the edge of the road.

"Take your foot off the gas," Erika said, "and change into reverse."

Erdogan did that.

"Right," said Erika, "now take your foot slowly off the clutch and drive backwards."

Erdogan did that as well and the car rolled backwards.

"Now," Erika said, "try again, but gently."

She'd learned that on the snowy slopes of the Rigi, she knew that in such situations the only hope was to keep calm. But the car didn't move, the tyres had no grip.

Erika got out and pushed with the whole force of her weighty body while Erdogan pressed the accelerator. The wheels rolled slowly over the shining ice and Erika got back in.

They drove across the plateau. There was a stiff wind from the north-west, snow drifts along the side of the road, but no problem with the surface itself.

Outside the village of Gempen there were sheep standing under an apple tree. When Erdogan stopped, they raised their heads and looked across at them with their narrow faces.

"Baah," Erdogan went, "*koyun.*" He pointed at the animals standing there staring, unmoving, then drove on.

They did the last bit to the inn on foot. The snow was knee-deep, it was colder up there, everything seemed whiter and more sparkling. The branches were bent down so low over the road that there was only a narrow strip of sky to be seen above. Like Christmas, Erika thought.

There was no question of climbing the tower to see the view. The snow was frozen hard on the iron struts and the platform at the top had almost disappeared in the swirl of flakes, so there was as good as nothing to be seen.

They stood by the revolving door at the bottom, which, it said, could be opened by inserting a one-franc piece. They looked up at the elegant iron structure, with the flakes falling on their faces. There was nothing to be seen of the green woods of the Jura heights, stretching away miles and miles to the west.

They walked over to the inn, shaking the snow off their coats in the vestibule before they went in. It was a large room with heavy wooden benches round the walls, and the one lamp over the round table in the middle was lit.

They sat down in its light. When the waitress came, a pretty young girl with shining blue eyes, they ordered the dish of the day: roast chicken with chips. Then they sat there waiting, suddenly tired, bewitched by their sudden wealth.

Shortly before four o'clock that Thursday afternoon a taxi stopped outside the Drei Könige Hotel and a young woman in a mock leopard-skin coat emerged. She had no luggage, no umbrella. And her outfit was anything but appropriate for the winter weather: high heels, sheer fishnet stockings, a coat which just about came down to her knees. She put her right leg on the granite kerb, pushed out her upper body in a nimble movement and, grasping the door for support, extricated her left leg and stood up. And all this she did with a radiant smile, like Aphrodite rising from the Aegean.

The hotel porter, who had been standing, miserable, behind the revolving door, presumably brooding over some sad family business – he looked as if family business for him couldn't be anything but sad – suddenly awoke, as if kissed by a ray of the sun. He pushed open the revolving door, rushed out, put up a large, black silk umbrella and, with a charming grin, held it over the young lady to protect her hair and imitation leopard skin. She nodded her thanks, told the taxi driver to wait a moment and, under the protection of the porter, swept through the revolving door into the hotel lobby.

Inside she gave him heartfelt thanks. Unfastening the top two buttons of her leopard-skin coat, she slipped her hand inside and brought out a yellow envelope, asking the porter to please take the letter to Monsieur Kayat without delay, he was anxious for it. Of course, the porter said, with the greatest pleasure. He took the envelope and sketched the brief bow of the Swiss.

The young woman thanked him in her sweet voice, carefully did up the top two buttons and had a quick glance round to see if there was a face she recognized in the lobby. There was none. Her eye rested a little longer on the lonely old bachelor sitting reading the newspaper on the couch behind the potted plant on the left, but she didn't seem to know him either. So she headed for the revolving door again, behind the porter. He set the door turning, almost too fast, it seemed, for the lady hesitated. Then she did go out and immediately the protective umbrella was held over her. With a smile of thanks she strutted on her high heels to the taxi, waited until the rear door was opened and, eyes lowered, placed her buttocks on the back seat. She drew in her legs with the fishnet stockings until her knees were nicely together, then looked, abruptly and totally surprisingly, up at the porter, who almost fell over. He swept his left hand up to his cap, grasped the car door and slammed it shut.

The car drove off through the snowflakes. For a while the rear lights could be seen, then they too faded.

The porter closed his umbrella. He had just experienced one of those moments which made his life in this poorly paid post worthwhile. There was a story behind the appearance of the young lady, that was immediately clear to him. There was an affair of the heart behind it, there was someone waiting, longing for a yellow envelope that would rescue him from the depths of loneliness and bear him up to a blissful paradise.

With fierce determination he set the revolving door in motion, went in, strode across the lobby, past the pot plant with the unobtrusive old fogey behind it, and stepped into the lift. He went up to the first floor, strode along the soft carpet of the corridor and stopped outside room 125. He knocked three times. Then he spoke, quietly and discreetly, almost in a whisper: "*Monsieur Kayat, il y a une lettre pour vous.*"

Kayat closed the door. That smutty porter. These sneaky Swiss. They all wanted to have a finger in the pie whenever they suspected there was a love affair or a lucrative bit of crooked business going on. Lickspittles the lot of them, crawling when confronted with real wealth or even just the pretence of it.

He sat down in the armchair beside the standard lamp, stuck a few potato chips in his mouth, enjoying the saltiness, the oily taste, then tore open the envelope. In it was a Syrian passport in the name of Assad Harif, a car key and confirmation from the car hire firm Stalder that a car with four-wheel drive and car phone awaited that same Assad Harif; it was ready for collection at any time, the bill had been paid. In addition there was the address and telephone number of the Basel Water Board and the sewage workers' changing room, a description of the sewage system of Badischer Station and a street map of the city on which a circle had been drawn round Hotel Rochat. No name of sender. No instructions. No orders. But Kayat knew what had to be done.

He went into the bathroom and ran a bath, then went over to the window. The snow hadn't stopped, the Rhine was steaming. It was a dull day outside. And the angler outside on the towpath, the man in the yellow anorak with his pipe in his mouth, who'd had his rod out over the river that morning, was back there, pointlessly, drearily, covered in snow. He or another fisherman would be standing there all evening, right through the night and the following day. They were out to catch a special fish, those gentlemen from Law & Order Inc.

Kayat got undressed and stood in front of the mirror. He was handsome, that was for sure, he was the way he wanted to be and he was one hundred per cent fit. If anyone could get those stones out of the sewers or the treatment plant, he was the man.

Later he went across the hotel lobby in his elegant camel-hair coat, not carrying anything, no briefcase, no suitcase, a good-looking, youngish businessman out to have a nice evening in the little city of Basel. The old fogey behind the pot plant noticed him immediately. Putting his newspaper away, he got up, went out through the revolving door and watched Kayat get into a taxi and drive off. He waved over a car that had been waiting across the road, got in and followed the taxi to Johanniterbrücke. There he saw Kayat get out and go into Trattoria Donati. He turned back. His expenses weren't so high that he could eat in the Donati. Anyway, the situation seemed clear to him.

Kayat sat down at the little table on the left, by the entrance. He ordered six *fine de claire* oysters, a *coquelet* with salad and a bottle of white wine from the Vaud, which he much enjoyed. Afterwards he took a walk across the snow-covered bridge to Lesser Basel, to a superior brothel he knew from previous visits, where he was well and most courteously served.

When he got back to the Drei Könige shortly after midnight, the old fogey was still there behind the pot plant, fast asleep. It's nice to be expected, Kayat thought, even better not to be abandoned. And how considerate the way they look after me.

That evening Peter Hunkeler drove out to Alsace with Hedwig. He was fed up, irritable and tired.

He had frittered away the rest of the morning with all sorts of minor stuff, reading the newspaper and making pointless telephone calls. At noon he'd made a brief visit to Harri's sauna. He'd twice had a lie-down in the steam room, a quarter of an hour each time. He'd lain down on his back, knees drawn up, like a baby in the womb, trying to think of nothing but the lovely heat all round him, oblivious to Huber, to Kayat, to diamonds. He could feel the sweat running out of his pores and dripping onto the towel he was lying on. During the second visit he'd even fallen asleep for a while, just a few minutes, as the sand-glass told him, but it had felt like an hour, a day, a year to him.

Afterwards he'd had some soup and sat out on the roof terrace. He'd watched the snowflakes falling onto the town, onto the terrace, onto his skin. The soft, cold way they floated had completely calmed him down.

In the afternoon he'd taken out the files again and studied them, but nothing new had struck him. Kayat had been on record for twelve years. He'd been arrested several times and held on remand, but nothing had come of it. Huber had been picked up at the Weil am Rhein border crossing with a high level of blood alcohol, but there was nothing remarkable about that. Weil was well known for its night-clubs and brothels, and it wasn't unusual for drunk Baselers to cross over after midnight to spend their Swiss francs on a bit of love. True, his alcohol content had been close to the upper limit, the point at which non-habitual drinkers were liable to have accidents, but that was no indication of professional criminality, of course.

There was nothing in the files about Zeugin, apart from one accusation of tax evasion amounting to 650,000 francs, but that hadn't got anywhere because the clever delaying tactics of the accused meant it had to be abandoned due to the statute of limitation.

So did that mean Dr Zeugin was a worthy citizen? Yes, going by what was in the files.

Hunkeler had locked the door of his office, taken the receiver off the telephone and put it on the desk in front of him. He'd pushed his chair back, braced his feet against the edge of the desk and spent half an hour thinking, eyes closed, in that state of semi-suspension. Then he'd given up, exhausted. Nothing at all worked. The case was hope-less without the diamonds. The only action he could take was to talk to Zeugin. But he was going to put that off until the next day.

Now he was sitting beside Hedwig at the wheel of his small car, driving along Hegenheimerstrasse, heading for the customs post. It had snowed continuously since the previous afternoon. The streets were icy, traffic almost at a standstill. The line of vehicles with their Alsace licence plates, the cars of the commuters who earned their valu-able Swiss francs in Basel and built their prefabs across the frontier with cheap French francs, was moving at walking pace, headlights on.

As always, there was no one at the French customs post, just the conscientious Swiss customs official standing outside, a steadfast snowman, on the lookout for someone who'd hidden a fillet of pork of more than a pound under the back seat and was trying to bring it in without paying customs duty.

Hunkeler had mixed feelings about these customs officers. He hated the way they stretched out their index fingers to force the cars to stop, the stony friendliness with which they asked about goods being carried. He was aware that there was something wild, mutinous, about himself that made them immediately suspicious when he appeared before their patriotic eyes and he was contemptuous of the submissiveness with which they bade the Herr Inspector drive on once they'd glanced at his identity card.

"Servile subjects, the lot of them," he would say, "the whole Helvetian freedom brigade. They should put the lot of them, standing to attention, on an iceberg that's floating south on the Atlantic and slowly melting."

Hedwig laughed. "Relax, we're in France now."

"It's just grotesque," he said, getting even more worked up. "That arsehole stands there outside in the snowstorm like our last Watch on the Rhine. At this time of the day everyone's driving out of Switzerland, no one's going in, but he's just too stupid to sit down in his little sentry box and read the newspaper." He gave a furious nod of his head. "What's the point of it anyway?" he went on. "The European Community's about to arrive, the borders are being opened but that guard dog there thinks he still has to defend Switzerland. Against whom then, against whom? Against General Bourbaki's French army fleeing the Prussians perhaps?"

He thumped the steering wheel, then had to slam his foot on the brake. The car skidded towards the side of the road and the engine stalled.

"That was a long speech," Hedwig said, "and a quick stop. But the fact is, you just have a short fuse."

Hunkeler was seething with rage. Fingers quivering, he turned the key in the ignition. It was the limit, that stupidity: a well-paid Swiss official standing out there in the falling snow watching more than twenty thousand French commuters drive back to Alsace. But when the police requested an extra man to give them at least a minimal chance of doing something about the drugs trade, the Treasury was down to its last centime. And if you got angry about that, because you were a man of morality and conscience, the woman who was kind enough to sleep with you now and then simply laughed at you and complained that you had a short fuse. He felt like really putting his foot down and sending the car smashing into the snowdrift on the other side of the icy bend. Of course he had a short fuse and he was going to keep it that way as long as possible.

The line of traffic split in Hegenheim, some cars turning left towards Hagenthal up in the hills while others went to the right, down onto the Rhine plain. It was all done in an amicable matter-of-fact manner Hunkeler couldn't help getting caught up in. And although he'd known the area for years, he suddenly enjoyed it as if he were seeing it for the first time.

In Hésingue, where they'd stopped at the only red light for miles around, he asked, "How are things at school?"

"Aha," she said, "you feel better now?"

"It was just something that occurred to me. Sorry."

"Six Turkish kids," she said, "three Spanish, four from somewhere in Yugoslavia, three from Vietnam, two from Greece, and all in the one class together with eight from Switzerland. How can you teach in a situation like that? One of the Greeks, a seven-year-old nipper, brought a knife – the kind that flicks out when you press a button – and one from Kosovo had a catapult, powerful enough to send a stone high over the school. He showed me."

"We used to have catapults as well," Hunkeler said, as he drove on when the light went green, and turned off towards Hügel. "We aimed at blackbirds and sparrows. Not at little tits and redstarts, but blackbirds and sparrows. We didn't have flick-knives. Why would we anyway?"

"I was wondering that too," Hedwig said.

"It's not our fault, we're not responsible."

"First of all they have to learn German," Hedwig said, "so that they can communicate in class and with me. But no one does anything about that."

"Of course not. They'll learn what they need to know themselves."

"No, it's a catastrophe. They're growing up in a no-man's-land, their only home is the TV."

"Right then," Hunkeler said, driving up the Stutz, being careful with his foot on the pedal so the wheels didn't spin, "let's assume it's a catastrophe. And now? Are we going out for a meal or not?"

"Of course we're going for a meal. What do you think? It's nothing to do with what we were talking about."

A bitter north-westerly was blowing across the plateau

at Trois Maisons. It was affecting the car, forcing it to the left, then suddenly letting up so that it almost slid into the snowdrifts on the right. It was like being in a boat on a storm-tossed sea, waking the sailor in Hunkeler. He steered gently and cautiously, keeping his eyes on the tail lights of the car in front as if it was a lighthouse. If an appropriate song had occurred to him, he would have been singing.

The house he'd bought three years ago (with cheap French francs) consisted of a half-derelict barn and a small cottage. There were two cats there when he parked outside it, tails erect and purring.

The living room was icy cold – it was more than two months since Hunkeler had last been there. Things had kept cropping up: a late operation in Rheingasse, a deadly boring meal with Schneeberger's friends for his birthday, or simply a beer in the Sommereck.

He fetched wood from the barn, where the wind was whistling, and carried it into the living room. He stuck some crumpled-up newspaper into the cast-iron stove and placed pine kindling on top. When that blazed up he took the lid off, dropped in some beech logs, then put it back on, leaving the door below open to make enough of a draught to keep the fire going. He could hear the flames in the stove and feel the heat from the solid cast iron spreading round the cold room; somewhere in the village he heard a dog bark. The stove was the focal point of the house, it was the hearth round which life settled on such a cold winter's evening.

He got up and half-closed the stove door, leaving it ajar so that the beech logs would burn down nice and slowly, spreading their increased warmth.

Hedwig was standing outside under the eaves, watching the cats eat.

"Come on," Hunkeler said, "let go to Jaeck's and have some wild boar *au poivre* with red cabbage, apples and chestnuts."

As they drove back from Jaeck's along the narrow road between the two villages, Hunkeler sang the lovely old song "Anchors away, my hearties", but he got no further than "golden stars" since he only knew the first few words. And anyway, he had to concentrate on the car to make sure the north-westerly didn't blow it off the road. It was just the way things had been when he was a boy sitting on the snow-plough drawn through the wintry splendour by the tractor.

The living room was nice and warm. Hunkeler added a few logs. Then they got into the high bed, embracing each other, warm and without a care in the world, as people have done through the ages on such dark nights.

The snow in Basel that night was the worst in living memory, covering streets and roofs, gardens and even the river. With no regard for borders, the flakes fell on the whole of the Rhine area, on the three sun-mountains called Belchen: the Belchen in the Jura, the Belchen in the Black Forest and the Belchen in the Vosges, as well as on the three moon-mountains called Blauen: the Blauen in the Vosges, the Blauen in the Black Forest and the Blauen in the Jura. The whole Upper-Rhine basin along with its surrounding hills was covered in snow, as if it was part of Greenland, and there were blue lights flashing through the streets.

It was really too much for the city's snow-clearing team. With difficulty they managed to keep the main routes open, but they couldn't clear the side streets anymore, the fall was too heavy. Moreover, a dozen or more trees had been uprooted by the weight of the snow, closing the streets to traffic. Even at midnight it was clear what chaos the morning would bring. Anyone who lived in one of the out-of-the-way streets in the suburbs, in one of those cute little houses with a room for handicrafts and the yawning boredom of a stale relationship, would either stay at home or arrive at their place of work two or three hours late. Only part of the machinery in workshops and factories would be in operation and teachers would be facing unusually small classes.

During the night, drug courier Guy Kayat got out of his bed in room 125 of the Drei Könige Hotel and went to the window. The Rhine was flowing past outside, its surface covered in thick snow. Nothing was to be séen on the opposite bank, not a tree nor a light. Nothing was to be seen on the narrow towpath below, no fisherman far and wide. Just one trail of human footprints could be seen in the twilight between the white of the snow and the dark of the night. Made by the stamp of heavy male feet, the tracks had been almost covered over by the snow, but the sharp edges were still clear enough. They were heading to the steps on the right that led up to the landing stage for boat trips.

Kayat stood there, motionless, for a quarter of an hour. Then he took a flashlight out of his travel bag, switched it on and placed it on the table in such a way that it sent its weak light from the window back into the room. He packed his belongings, got dressed, pocketed the passport in the name of Assad Harif, slipped into his camel-hair coat and put on a black-and-white-check peaked cap. Then he went to the door out onto the terrace, lifted the bag up over the balustrade and dropped it. It made a soft landing in a little puff of snow.

Shutting the door behind him, Kayat climbed over the balustrade, grasped the drainpipe in both hands, pushed himself out from the wall with both feet and slid down. It hurt his fingers – the pipe was ice-cold – but he got down safely. Picking up his bag, he brushed off the snow and fol-lowed the man's footsteps up to the landing stage.

A truck drove past, its heavy snowplough striking sparks from the road surface. There was a taxi waiting, covered in snow. The driver was asleep.

Kayat woke him, got in and told the man, who was swear-ing and cursing, to take him to Stalder car hire.

It took a long search to find his car. The licence plates were all covered in snow and he had to wipe several clear before he found the right one. It was a small red car with an aerial. He got in, closed the door, and stuck his hands into his pockets against his warm thighs. Once he'd got some feeling back, he switched on the engine and the windshield wipers. He selected four-wheel drive, registering with satis-faction the jolt in the gearbox.

The car managed to get over the wall of snow created by the snowplough, though it did skid a little. Then it went smoothly along the cleared road and across Mittlere Brücke to Lesser Basel and, after a few detours along the maze of one-way streets, stopped outside Badischer Station.

Kayat smoked a cigarette and looked across at the main gate, which was closed. There were no lights on, the concourse was in deepest darkness, the trains weren't running yet.

He took out the street map that was in the yellow envelope the concierge had given him, concentrating on the three crosses marking the access points to the sewers outside the station. In the explanation they were called "iron drain covers that can be lifted off with a pickaxe or a strong car jack, if not bolted down".

Kayat shook his head. What were they thinking about, these desk-bound crooks! Presumably they imagined, sitting there at their desks, whisky glass in their right hand, cigar in their left, that it was a pleasure scraping away like a dog at drain covers in the middle of the night. And what did "if not bolted down" mean? If they were actually bolted down you'd need a wrench that fitted. But where could you find a wrench that fitted? And assuming he did manage to find one of the marked drain covers, what then? He still wouldn't know how to find the connection to Badischer Station in the dark pipes.

He didn't feel at all like going down into this underworld, that wasn't his territory. Always try to be the one to determine the time and place of unavoidable conflict – that had been one of the basic rules he'd learned in his profession, and he didn't like the look of things down there.

For a moment he thought of going straight across the border to Mulhouse and hiding there until the dust had settled. Those blasted stones were bad news for him. He'd sensed that back in the train, most of all – he wished he'd flushed them away there and then. If he had, he wouldn't have had to run across the station concourse to the men's toilets, pursued by a gaggle of cops, and he wouldn't have had the Basel police pestering him.

The others were dangerous enough. The others who wanted their jewels back, the others who had him in their clutches, whether in Basel or Mulhouse or anywhere else.

Suddenly he froze in terror, his mouth dry as sand. There was a blue light turning out of a side street, a second one behind it, then a third. The lights were heading for the station, straight towards him. What was he doing here? How could he explain why he was here outside the closed gate to the station at this early hour? He realized that his hand with the cigarette was trembling, his throat tickling. He bent over the steering wheel and coughed three times, a hacking cough that brought tears to his eyes.

Then he heard the loud roar of powerful engines. He sat up and watched, stunned, as three powerful trucks with high, shiny snowploughs and revolving blue lights lined up next to each other, then glided past and, clanking and grating, pushed the snowdrift to one side.

He waited until the trucks had gone. Then he opened the side window, threw out the cigarette that he'd smoked down to the filter and took out the description of the sewage workers' changing room. It would surely be quiet there now and there wouldn't be any bolted-down drain covers, any stinking pipes. He'd go and have a look in there, he simply had to do something.

He found the changing room right away. No one was worried about someone breaking in, no one had seen to it that it had strong bolts. The aluminium lockers the height of a man were along the right-hand wall. Kayat shone his flashlight on them, then broke open three and checked the contents. It was pointless, they contained nothing but worn underwear, dirty sweaters, stinking socks. Kayat examined the nameplates stuck on them and noted down five names: two of the workers were clearly from Italy, two were Yugoslavs and one was called Erdogan Civil.

Kayat went out of the changing room, shutting the door in a rough-and-ready way – the fact that there'd been a break-in couldn't be kept secret anyway. He got in his car, drove back over to Greater Basel and parked outside the Hotel Rochat on Petersgraben. A room had been reserved in his new name. He asked for the Basel & District telephone directory and went up in the lift. Shattered, he was longing for a good sleep.

Lying on the bed, he looked up the names he'd noted down. He found three: the two Italians, who had the same number, and Erdogan Civil, who lived on Lörracherstrasse.

Peter Hunkeler was having a dream. It was by the Altachenbach, the stream near where he'd grown up in the countryside south of Basel. The stream had been his home ever since he could remember: the watercourse that sought a new way through the banks of mud after every summer storm, the fine-veined sheets of ice in the winter with the thin layer of snow on them, the black leeches on the bottom – he never dared take one in his hand.

It was by that stream, under the bridge, with its musty smell and all sorts of rubbish that no one wanted anymore lying around. Among it was a woven-leather belt someone must have just thrown away. It lay there in a strange light, unreal, like something out of a fairy tale, but very real despite that, as if it belonged in a different, more real world. And it was there for him, for Peter Hunkeler, for the child he had once been and in some mysterious way now was once more. Faced with his find he didn't dare move, he was afraid it might disappear at any moment, slip away, winding like a snake. Then he heard a sound, a sound calling him from far, far away, from a distant cave, perhaps, that was nothing to do with him at that moment. There was the belt, the important thing was to get hold of it. But there was that sound again.

Hunkeler woke up. He heard the telephone ringing in the hall outside, heard it stop and start eight times until he realized it was for him.

Pushing Hedwig's leg off his, he got out of the warm bed, went out into the ice-cold hall and lifted the receiver. It was Madörin.

"Are you crazy?" Hunkeler asked. "What time is it anyway?"

"Almost seven," Madörin said. "I'm sorry, but a few things have happened that you might find interesting."

"I had a dream," Hunkeler said, "but I'm not going to tell you what it was. There was a belt of woven leather in it. It was like an animal and it was for me."

"Oh do wake up," Madörin said. "You can go back to your dream later. Now listen: firstly, someone's broken into the sewage workers' changing room on Hochbergerstrasse. Someone's been through three of the lockers. That was last night."

"Broken in," Hunkeler said, "well, well." He could feel the cold on the bare soles of his feet working its way up his body. Through the barred window in the front door he could see it was dark outside.

"Yes," Madörin said. "The nightwatchman noticed it and called the police."

86

"I was fast asleep," Hunkeler said, yawning. He could hear Hedwig turning over in the bedroom and starting to snore again.

"Do you think I enjoy calling you to disturb your sleep?" Madörin said caustically.

"Sorry. It's still the dead of night out here and everything's dead quiet as well."

Madörin ignored that. "Secondly, Kayat's disappeared."

"What d'you mean, disappeared?" Hunkeler suddenly felt he needed a pee, he could hardly hold it back.

"Are you fully awake now?"

"Yes, I am awake!" Hunkeler shouted into the phone. "What d'you mean, disappeared?"

"When I heard about the break-in I immediately called Schneeberger in the Drei Könige. He was sitting in the lobby and had clearly nodded off for a moment. He went to have a look in Room 125. It was empty – cleared out, the bird had flown."

"And Haller?" Hunkeler asked at once in a sharp voice.

"He was on the towpath down by the Rhine until two. Then the snow must have got too much for him, so he went home for a couple of hours to have a coffee and get warmed up."

"Have you all gone out of your tiny minds?" Hunkeler exclaimed. "Right round the clock, I told you, not for as long as you feel like it."

He could hear Hedwig muttering something in her dream.

"There are those in their double bed in their country cottage," Madörin said nastily, "while others are standing outside in the snowy night. What do you think of that?"

"Right," said Hunkeler. "I'll be in Hochbergerstrasse in an hour's time."

Putting the receiver down, he opened the front door, went out and had a piss in the brightly gleaming snow. He was trembling. Over in the shed a cow coughed, a dull, forced cough. The sky was jet-black, dotted with glittering stars. It was icy cold. In the east a streak of grey announced dawn.

When Hunkeler set off with Hedwig half an hour later it was already light in the village. The sound of the milking machine was coming from the cowshed; inside the steaming beasts were standing side by side, their dripping mouths munching hay, pressing heavy pats of dung out of their rears, every one of their bodies a warming stove.

The road up the hill was so icy the car couldn't manage it. Hunkeler looked for his gloves in the glove compartment. They weren't there. "My God" was the only curse that occurred to him. He got out, dragged the snow chains from the trunk and started fitting them on the front wheels. His annoyance turned to pure despair as he pulled the ice-cold chains on over the hard rubber only for them to fall off minutes later. "Never again a policeman," he heard Hedwig saying in the car, "never again your friend and helper."

Hunkeler was livid. He got out again, slamming the door so hard the bodywork almost fell apart. He slipped and nearly fell over when he bent to pick up the chains. Kneeling, panting, in the snow, he managed to fit the chains on the wheels, so that he could thread the hooks into the eyelets and fasten them with the rubber rings. When he got back in, Hedwig was sitting there like a mummy, looking straight ahead.

Once he was driving across the plateau, the pure, virgin snowfields on either side, the engine finally started to warm up. The stars had long since disappeared, there was a flush of pink in the east: it was a crystal-clear February morning. The lights of the airport down on the plain were still on. Beyond them lay the city with the high administration buildings of the chemical works and, a little further to the right, the dark towers of the old town. A beautiful sight, Hunkeler thought, almost where I belong.

Erdogan Civil heard the jangling of the alarm clock. He stayed curled up, sensing Erika's body moving slightly against his back. The jangling stopped.

He kept his eyes shut and continued breathing steadily. He remembered a dream he'd had, something about a hoe he'd lost in his father's field when he still had to hoe the field so that it could be sown. But it wasn't just about the hoe and the field, there was something else, something much more important about it. Suddenly the handle of the hoe had turned into a snake that moved and bit his left hand.

He tried to move his left hand – there was no problem, it was unharmed. It had all been just a dream.

He was used to dreaming the craziest things, above all in the early morning, once the weariness of the night had gone. Then, as he woke up, he was happy to feel Erika's body beside him. The dreams couldn't spoil that.

He turned over onto his other side, stretched and yawned. The handle of a hoe turning into a snake – what a load of nonsense.

He'd seen enough snakes on the delta of the river when he was a boy and had to watch over the few cows his father possessed. He recalled the thin grass on the sandbanks, the knee-deep water where the cows stood to cool off in the heat, the flamingos out in the lagoon with their pink feathers and hooked beaks that dipped like lightning into the silvery shoals of fish. And then he remembered the diamonds lying on the table.

Those stones were less real than the craziest of dreams: a handful of pebbles like polished drops of water that had dropped out of a filthy pipe, a shining glitter of blue amid all the rubbish, dribbling down at his feet and into his hand. It was as if a star had fallen from the night sky into the lagoon, right in the middle of the flamingos as they spent the night there on their spindle-shanks.

He'd had a bit of good luck, a great piece of undeserved good fortune for once in his life – a kiss from heaven – and he was so happy and afraid that he didn't dare move.

The telephone rang. He sat up and watched, uncomprehending, as Erika came from the kitchen, went to the phone and answered it.

"Yes," she said, "Erdogan Civil does live here. One moment, please."

She put the receiver down and whispered, "A man. He wants to speak to you, a foreigner, not a Swiss."

Erdogan got up and put the receiver to his ear. "Yes?"

He heard a calm, firm man's voice, "Listen, you poor Turkish devil, you work in the sewers, don't you?"

"Yes," Erdogan said, his hand trembling.

"Don't worry," the voice said, "I'm not going to hurt you. I just want to pass on some information. I've lost a handful of diamonds. Very beautiful, worth a lot of money. They're in the sewers near Badischer Station and if you should find them you must know that they belong to me. And that I want them back. Understood?"

"No," Erdogan said, "they belong to me."

Horrified, he transferred the receiver to his other hand that was trembling less.

"Aha," the voice said, "so you've found them."

"No," Erdogan shouted, "I've no idea what you're talking about."

"Oh yes you have. I can well understand that you'd like to keep them. Who wouldn't like to have a handful of diamonds in times like this, eh?" There was amusement in the voice and it didn't sound unfriendly. "But that's not possible, unfortunately. Those diamonds don't belong to you but to me. Understood?"

"Will you stop going on at me, please?" Erdogan begged. "Who are you anyway?"

"That's nothing to do with it," the voice said, casually, as if they'd been talking about the weather. "I'm a friend, you see. And friends don't steal from each other, surely you realize that, don't you? Otherwise I'll have to punish you. You live with a woman, don't you, my friend? Think it over, but not for too long. I'll be getting back to you. All the best, my friend – and no police. Understood?"

He could hear the other man's breath, clearly puffing out tobacco smoke. "Understood?"

"Yes," Erdogan whispered.

"Good. I'm stronger than you. Much stronger, you have to understand that." He hung up.

Erdogan stood there, barefoot in his pyjamas, the receiver

in his hand, looking at Erika, who'd been listening without a word. From the carpenter's came the sound of the circular saw, a high, whirring noise; there was the scent of coffee in the room, a strong, bitter smell.

"Put the receiver down," Erika said, going into the kitchen. Erdogan could hear her busying herself there. She reappeared with the breakfast tray, which she set on the table, pushing the diamonds to one side. "Do put that phone back down," she said, "and come and have something to eat."

Erdogan put the telephone down, carefully, as if something might get broken. He sat down, picked up the cup of coffee Erika had poured for him, took a swig.

"Who was that?" she asked.

"That was a man who knows I've got the diamonds. He wants them back and he said he was stronger than me."

She spread some pâté on the bread, slowly and precisely. "There, you see," she said, "nothing will come of it."

Erdogan watched as she ate the bread. Like a sheep, he thought, that has no idea of anything, like a stupid *koyun* chewing the cud.

"Why are you giving me that stupid look?" she asked. "I told you right from the beginning nothing would come of it."

Erdogan shook his head, again and again. "How does he know? Where did he get my name?"

She spread another slice of bread and pushed it over to him. "Eat," she said, "and drink your coffee, that'll wake you up. Then you can call the police."

"No," Erdogan said, "I'm not going to do that."

"Do you know what you said to that man on the telephone just now," she asked, "do you remember?"

Erdogan picked up the bread spread with pâté and took a bite. It tasted like sand.

"You said, 'No, they belong to me,' so you've told him that you've got them."

"Oh do stop criticizing me, OK? Help me instead."

She poured some more coffee. "You're far too stupid to deal with them," she said, "you've no chance at all. And there's something I want to make quite clear to you. I don't want to lose you because of these stupid diamonds. Do you understand that?"

"That's my business," he said, "men's business. You know nothing about that."

He said it as firmly as he could. He looked at her, eyes screwed up, and he saw her face suddenly go white, white as snow.

He got up, fetched a plastic bag from the kitchen, took a clean handkerchief out of the chest of drawers and went to the table. He carefully dropped the diamonds onto the handkerchief, tied it up in a bundle and put it in the plastic bag. Erika watched him without a word, the colour returning to her face. She started to spread pâté on the rolls for his lunch.

Once he was dressed he took the rolls and stood there in front of her. She was still in her dressing gown, hair uncombed, lips greasy, it seemed to him. "That's my business," he said again, "men's business." He went out.

The stairs were empty as usual: flecks of plaster on the steps, damp patches on the walls, a smell of cold and dust. He had to wait for a moment in the passage at the bottom as a forklift truck loaded with planks drove past.

It was light outside. The road seemed to be shining with all the snow. It was trodden down on the pavement and road, piled up on top of the parked cars. There were only a few people around, the cars were going at walking pace. A tram went past at the crossing two houses further on, its windows steamed up. There was nothing unusual to be seen, only the snow was new.

The American car was across the road, the red soft top couldn't be seen at all. Erdogan waited a moment in the shadow of the doorway. No one noticed him, no unknown man came up to him, knife drawn. He looked up at the bright gleam of the sky.

He climbed over the snow piled up in the gutter and went across to the car. He managed to release the frozen front door and pull it open. He got in and turned the starter several times. The engine spluttered a bit but didn't start, it was too cold.

Erdogan got out and went over to the bicycle park where his moped was, fixed his bag on the luggage rack, started the engine and got into the saddle. He drove carefully over the crossing, keeping his feet on the road surface in case the wheels started to skid.

He looked neither to the right nor to the left. The road surface was icy. He wouldn't be able to get away if he was being followed anyway. If there was someone after him, then he just had to put his trust in Allah. He had to get through this and he was determined to do everything necessary to hang on to the diamonds.

Peter Hunkeler was driving across to Lesser Basel. He'd just dropped Hedwig off outside St Johann school. He'd briefly glanced across at the playground where the kids were running around in the snow in red and yellow plastic jackets. Then he'd been astonished to find that Hedwig had her arms round him and was kissing him. That was what was so marvellous about her, he thought, the way she could surrender so completely to her moods.

He drove past the site of the old City Gardens Department where years ago young people had established an independent youth centre. It had worked well but had been unauthorized and rejected in a plebiscite by the narrow-minded middle-class majority. And the police had shut it down.

Back then Hunkeler would have refused if he'd been ordered to take part in that operation, for he knew that his daughter Isabelle had been involved. How could he have driven his daughter out?

But that was the way things were, that was the way his life was. He was a member of the Basel police and the Basel police were commanded by old fogeys who believed above all else in maintaining the established order and the power of the older generation.

In this town, he thought, the police were no longer an instrument of democratic power that could be used to protect minorities – young people, for example; the police had become an instrument of the powerful majority that was used to suppress minorities under the pretext of authority.

He turned off onto Dreirosenbrücke. There was still ice on the carriageway, but it wasn't gleaming anymore, it was dull, either from the salt that had been spread, or from the warmth of the exhaust fumes and of the early morning. The sky wasn't as clear as it had been over Trois Maisons. There were streaks of white up there, thin strips of cloud, the first sign of the warmth to come.

The bridge was congested in both directions, one truck behind another, in both lanes, each one with a trailer – huge monsters with belching exhausts, their tarpaulins bearing inscriptions in French, German and Scandinavian, some with chains on their drive-wheels. It was a transport armada of enormous tonnage, laden with refrigeration units, chemicals, spare parts. Among them were car transporters with a dozen new models sitting tilted behind them – another fresh consignment of vehicles for the ever more senseless motor traffic.

Hunkeler switched the engine off. That was the regulation to protect the environment. In no way did he believe the measure was effective but it did soothe his conscience a little.

Why should he feel guilty, actually? Everyone drove a car, even though everyone was against them in principle. Should he perhaps have gone out to Alsace by bicycle – in this cold, in this snow? And anyway, was he responsible for the environment? Would not using the car have had any effect? No, it would have had no effect at all.

He tried to relax. "I am calm and relaxed," he murmured, "and my left hand is heavy and warm." He didn't get any further. Those things he was supposed to say bored him stiff.

He closed his eyes and saw a pond in the woods by the river. He'd been going for a walk when Isabelle was six or seven. They'd driven out to Kembs together and parked the car on the island between the ship canal and the old Rhine. Then they'd walked along the old course of the river, their ears filled with the noise from the engines of the vehicles on the German autobahn on the other side, their eyes on the rippling water. It was evening, a warm summer's evening, the birds were whistling and singing and three herons had flown up the river. He could remember it clearly, he could still see their widespread wings in the sky above him, their beaks stretched out in front and their long skinny legs trailing, because it had been an image of unbelievable, hardly comprehensible beauty.

Later they'd come across a pond, a stretch of quiet, still water, separated from the course of the river by a mudbank with willows growing on it. There were lots of bits of paper and plastic on the twigs and branches, evidence of the height of a flood.

The water in the pond was as clear as glass. Every plant growing in it could be seen, even the algal bloom was bright green, as if it had blossomed in a palm house. Every fish could be seen as clearly as if it were in an aquarium. And quite close to the bank there was a leech, a black worm, as unmoving as if it were a piece of wood, coming from a childhood dream.

Isabelle asked if she could go in. He nodded. She took off her shoes, tucked up her skirt, then waded round in the pond for at least a quarter of an hour, her pleasure clear to see, carefully taking one step after another, looking across to her father on the bank again and again to make sure he was watching.

He watched, captivated. He saw his daughter walking across that transparent mirror reflecting the sky, the water plants shining, saw the way her steps made slight waves across the surface, making the sky and the plants sway, and he realized that he loved that child above all else.

Then she'd come back to the bank and put her shoes back on, without a word. As night fell they'd walked back to the car, the two of them, mute as fishes.

Since that evening Hunkeler's attitude towards his daughter had been one of reserve, shyness even. He had withdrawn from her because he had realized that this young woman didn't belong to him anymore. That evening alone remained with him, that quarter of an hour by the water with the rippling mirror.

Since then he had lost touch with Isabelle. She had studied design in Munich, then come back to Basel and worked in an advertising agency. When the old city garden site was occupied she had been involved from the very beginning and devoted all her time and energy to it, unpaid of course.

After it had been cleared and destroyed she had gone abroad. Once Hunkeler had received a postcard from Greece, sent from the island of Ithaca, where she seemed to be living with a gang of latterday hippies in a tent by a watercourse where eels and turtles lived, as she wrote.

Hunkeler opened his eyes again. What's the point of immersing myself in the past, he thought, dreaming like this until the water comes dripping out of all the joins in my memory? I'm a policeman, I'm on the side of those in power and I've lost my daughter for good.

He had to live with that and he knew it. He had simply conformed; he'd had to conform. What else could he have done? How else could he have earned the money for his family, for his wife and child? "What care I for wife or child?" he said to himself, with a wicked grin at quoting a line from a Heine poem he'd been forced to learn off by heart. Should he perhaps have become a *clochard* in Paris, a drunkard with hat, coat and bottle of wine, spending the night on the grille over the Métro air vent or under one of the bridges? Or would it have been better for him to become a welfare case in peaceable Switzerland, one of the homeless with a strong character and an unbridled desire for freedom, but no money, one who'd fallen out of the social network, as it was called in officialese, harassed and driven off by the police?

No, he wouldn't have been able to do that, he didn't have the strength of will, he was too weak. And the day would come when even Isabelle would have to conform. Whether he or she liked it was irrelevant. When she had a child, at the latest, she'd be compelled to slot back into society and accept the rules of the game. No one brings up a child beside a stream on a Greek island in the company of eels and turtles, he thought, she will have to come back, and she will.

He realized how bored he was with his thoughts, but he had no others available, he had to take those that occurred to him, however reactionary, however hopeless they were. Better to be reactionary and honest rather than dissembling and progressive, he thought, and at that he felt almost like puking with rage at what he'd been thinking. Who was he, then? Was he really the last little pile of shit on God's earth?

He heard the whine of the truck in front of him, a cloud of soot came out of the exhaust. Then the vehicle started and the line of traffic began to move.

It was shortly before eight when Hunkeler drew up outside the sewage workers' changing room on Hochbergerstrasse.

Madörin was there, and Haller, drinking coffee out of disposable cups. Beside them were several men in their work clothes. One was called Berger. He was the foreman and he introduced his colleagues: Luigi Violi, Sandro Berzoni, Duro Sepanovic. Two were still absent; presumably they'd been held up by the snow.

"Where's Schneeberger?" Hunkeler asked.

"He's sitting, as instructed, in the lobby of the Drei Könige Hotel," Heller reported, clearly and dutifully.

"Is he? And what's he doing there?"

"Perhaps Kayat will come back," Haller said, "you never know."

"Perhaps he'll have forgotten something and come to collect it. Is that what you mean?"

Haller took his pipe out of his pocket and made a show of scraping it clean. "Don't go on at me. I know I've been an arsehole but it was damn cold."

"What?!" Hunkeler shouted. "It was what?"

"It was damn cold. Not a soul about anywhere. Just snow. It drives you round the bend."

"You're two damn arseholes, that's what you are." Hunkeler turned away and spat in the snow. "Are there any tracks?"

"Yes. Somehow he managed to jump down from the balcony. I found the print of his bag in the snow."

"Right. You go and get Schneeberger from the Drei Könige and tell him he's to check out all the hotels in Basel for Kayat – he'll probably have changed his name."

Haller emptied the scrapings from his pipe into his disposable cup and dumped it in the trash can. Then he walked out without a word. He clearly felt insulted.

Turning to Berger, the foreman, Hunkeler asked, "Has anything been stolen?"

"No, nothing," he replied. "I can't see the point of the business. Perhaps it was a druggie looking for the price of his next shot. In my opinion, they should all be put up against a wall."

"Just stop it. I don't want to hear that anymore."

Berger looked at him in astonishment. "But you're from the police."

"Yes, I'm from the police," Hunkeler shouted, "and no one's going to be put up against a wall here. Understood?"

"Calm down," Madörin said, "he didn't mean it that way. Also, three lockers have been forced open. Just three, not all of them. That's odd."

Hunkeler pulled out a cigarette but didn't light it. In what way had the guy meant it then, the idiot? "Right," he said, "let's have a look, then, and see what's in the two other lockers."

Berger fetched a chisel and forced open the doors with no problem at all. Madörin rummaged round inside and brought out dirty underwear.

"That one belongs to Miroslav Ivanovic," Berger said, "and that one to Erdogan Civil."

"A Turk?" Hunkeler asked.

"Yes, a good worker, quiet and reliable. Yesterday he was absent for the first time."

"Why?" Hunkeler asked.

"He phoned to say he had toothache."

"Let's say someone drops a wristwatch in the toilet. It's washed down into the sewers. Is it possible one of the workers might find it?"

Berger nodded. "You'd never believe the kind of things we've found: keys, wedding rings, false teeth."

"And diamonds?" Hunkeler asked.

"I should be so lucky. Things like that tend to get stuck at particular places where two pipes aren't aligned, overlapping."

"Overlapping?" Hunkeler asked.

Berger put his hands together so that the tips of his right-hand fingers were over the nails of his left. "Like that, a little barrage."

"Has anyone found diamonds at a barrage like that?"

Berger screwed up his eyes. "Why diamonds?"

"It could be," Madörin broke in, "that someone flushed some diamonds down the toilet in Badischer Station, for example."

Berger shook his head with a laugh. "Diamonds in the shit, that would be something. What d'you think, Luigi?"

Luigi shook his head, laughing too. Then the laugh disappeared from his lips and he looked thoughtful. "This morning," he said, "while I was still asleep, someone I didn't know phoned and asked where I'd hidden the diamonds."

"Yes," the other Italian said, "some arsehole. He woke us when we were fast asleep."

"And you?" Hunkeler asked the Yugoslav. "Did someone call you as well?"

"No. Sorry, I haven't got a phone. But I am registered, according to the rules. It's all there."

A moped pulled up outside. There was a short man on it wearing a red helmet. He got off, took out the ignition key, then, sticking a plastic bag on the carrier, he picked up his lunchbox and came in. He looked round in surprise when he saw the strangers. "Sorry," he said, "I know I'm late. The snow."

He went over to his locker. "Why is it open?"

"That's Erdogan Civil," Berger said.

Twisting his cigarette between his finger and thumb, Hunkeler said, "Pleased to meet you. How's the toothache, Herr Civil? Better, I hope."

The little man hesitated. He took off his helmet; it had left a red mark on the top of his forehead. "Better, thank you."

"Where exactly did it hurt?" Hunkeler said.

Erdogan opened his mouth and pointed to the top back left. "There."

Madörin took the little man's bag and emptied it. Three sandwiches packed in aluminium foil fell out; a bottle of beer rolled onto the floor but didn't break.

"Rolls," Erdogan said, "with smoked sausage pâté. What is it you want?"

"There was a break-in here last night," Hunkeler explained, "and we're wondering why. Do you know? I'm Peter Hunkeler, by the way, and I'm an inspector with the Basel police. Have you any idea what someone might have been looking for here?"

"No. There's nothing to steal here. We're as poor as the sewer rats." Wrinkling his forehead and looking at the bottle of beer on the floor, he said, "May I put my things back in my bag?"

Bending down, Madörin picked up the bottle. "We'll do that. Sorry. But what's this? Are you allowed to drink beer, being a Turk, I mean? Or are you a Christian?"

"No, a Muslim. But I drink what I want and what does me good."

Hunkeler patted him on the back. "You're right there. Allah looks at the souls of people, not in their bellies, isn't that so?"

The little man looked at him uncomprehending, turned away and took off his coat.

"Anyway," Hunkeler said, "did a man call you this morning and ask about some diamonds?"

"No, of course not."

"Why did you say 'of course not'?" Madörin barked. "Why not simply 'no'?"

"I've no idea what you're getting at," the little man said. "Sorry."

Berger tapped the side of his head. "I've just remembered something. After work yesterday evening Herr Civil had to go back down again. The connection from Badischer Station was blocked. Civil opened it up again."

Putting his cigarette between his lips, Hunkeler lit it. "Well? And what did you find?"

Erdogan thought for a long time, slowly shaking his head. Then he seemed to remember. "Yes, I was down there. There were diapers and stuff like that. And there was a green woman's dress, if that's the kind of thing you mean. It was torn and covered in shit." He stood there as if he had nothing more to say, eyes down, almost obsequious. He wasn't happy, that much was clear, but who does feel happy when they're being interrogated by the police?

Hunkeler hesitated. It could all be mere coincidence, the blocked pipe, his toothache, the break-in. He looked at the men standing round him in the room. They had good faces, they weren't criminals, and if one of them should have the good fortune to find a handful of diamonds, then good luck to him.

"Listen," Madörin said, legs apart, hips forward, jaw jutting in the typical police threat-posture, ridiculous but also dangerous, "just you listen to me, Herr Civil. If you think you can tell us tall stories, you're very much mistaken. We're not in Turkey here, in this country we tell the straight, honest truth. You're a seasonal worker, aren't you?"

The little man raised his eyes. "I'm an honest man, I speak the truth, believe me."

Hunkeler stubbed out his cigarette, taking his time until it was completely out. "The fact is," he began, "that a consignment of high-carat diamonds disappeared from Badischer Station, presumably down the toilet, therefore into the sewers. These diamonds are the profit from drugs. Which means that they belong to people who deal in drugs on a grand scale. They are criminals who will do anything – and that means murder, Herr Civil."

"No," the little man said, "I've got nothing to do with drugs."

"That's not what I'm saying. But if you do happen to have found the diamonds, which is quite possible, isn't it – you do find wedding rings and false teeth now and then, don't you? – if you do happen to have found the diamonds, you're in great danger. Do you understand?"

Erdogan sat down on the bench, putting his head in both hands. "That's the toothache coming back," he said, "up there on the left. It throbs with every heartbeat."

"If you say so," Hunkeler said. "If you change your mind, call us. Perhaps we'll come and see you, in your home, I mean. Where do you live?"

"Lörracherstrasse. I haven't got anything hidden at home."

"Where then?" Madörin barked.

Erdogan looked up. "It would be lovely to find some diamonds. Then I'd be a rich man and not have to clean shitty pipes in a foreign country."

"What do you mean by that?" Madörin said, taking a step forward.

"I mean that, not having found any diamonds, I'll have to keep on cleaning shitty pipes, unfortunately."

"Stop it," Hunkeler said to Madörin, "you're not supposed to intimidate people. We'll proceed as follows: you'll go down with one of the men to the connection pipe from Badischer Station."

"Why does it have to be me?" Madörin moaned.

"Someone has to do it. And you," he said turning to Berger, "will see to it that new locks are fitted here."

He went out onto the forecourt. He felt tired, worn out. In front of him was a moped, an old model with a torn saddle and a plastic bag with an advert for a brand of cigarettes over the back. Hunkeler got into his car.

Erika Waldis served the last customer of the morning, an old man who'd bought a loaf of Basel bread, a quarter pound of butter and a packet of budgerigar food. She closed the till and took out the key. The clock in the entry hall, where trolleys had been left all over the place, showed the time as twelve-thirty. The lights were switched off, the shelves in the half-light looked as gloomy as in a pine forest.

Standing up straight, she lifted her arms as high as she could and stood on tiptoe for five seconds. Then she slowly squatted down, trying to keep her heels on the floor all the time, also for five seconds. That's what she'd learned during therapy.

She stood up again, with difficulty – she simply weighed too much. She was well aware of that, she didn't need a doctor to tell her. But how could she lose weight when she was sitting on that chair all day, registering the prices of sausages and noodles?

By now the entrance hall was empty as well. Erika started to push the trolleys together until they were in two straight lines next to each other. That wasn't her job, but she hated any disorder.

She went up the stairs to the self-service restaurant, picked up a tray and cutlery and joined the line. Today there was roast chicken with chips, beef stew with mashed potatoes and, as on every Wednesday in winter, black pudding and liver sausage with sauerkraut. Erika chose the beef stew. Antonio, in his white cap, gave her a wink as he dug a pit in the mash with his ladle.

She found an empty table by the window that looked out over a flat roof. In warmer weather there were tables out there with sunshades. Now it was covered in snow that had a dull shimmer in the hazy grey light.

She knew a few of the customers in the restaurant by sight, though she gave them no more than a nod. They were men who lived on their own, men with frayed collars and faded silk ties from Luino on Lake Maggiore. They were in their Sunday best, as they were every lunchtime, even though it wasn't Sunday. They were sitting there, each on his own, carefully cutting the meat up into little chunks and taking a long time chewing it, their necks skinny and wrinkled, their eyes lowered. Beside them were the widows, in twos and threes, talking quietly, they didn't want to be a nuisance to anyone. They had also dressed up, as well as they could, with neatly ironed blouses and all kinds of old-fashioned hats on their heads.

Erika was happy to be sitting by herself. She needed time to think things over. She was frightened by what had happened that morning.

Men's business, she thought, what is that, men's business? What does that idiot, nothing more than a big child, actually mean by it? Does he really think he's capable of dealing with the man on the telephone by himself?

He had his fantasies, did Erdogan – her Erdogan, in Switzerland he belonged to her. Basically, he was like all the other men she'd known. The difference was that she loved him. She'd no idea why, she simply loved him and that was that. But he was just like all the others, nothing but a big child, a boy. Hardly had he got a whiff of money than this otherwise very gentle man had been filled with the fighting spirit. Without hesitation he would risk everything – his love, his skin, his life – even though any sensible person could see at once that he didn't have a chance. If only he'd at least been willing to talk about the problem, weigh up the various possibilities, develop a plan of action.

If he intended to keep the diamonds at all costs, then he should at least have hidden them where no one would find them. For example, the sand on the bottom of the aquarium would have been a good place. But no, he stuck his booty under his arm and drove around with it. And if she made any objection he was as obstinate as a billy goat refusing to go into the pen.

They were sitting over there, all those stupid, old, pig-headed guys who'd come down in the world, every one of them alone, isolated, worn out. Just you have a look at them, Erdogan my dear, and see where they've ended up, fighters that they were. Nothing but old ninnies, still trying to pretend they're strong, elegant men. And they're nothing but a bundle of misery.

Shortly after one, by which time the restaurant was half-empty, Nelly came over to her table.

"I just wanted to see how you are," she said. "Have you recovered?"

Erika hesitated. "I wasn't ill," she said. "I've had problems."

"With Erdogan?"

"Yes. He found some diamonds in the sewers and won't hand them over, the chump."

"Diamonds in the sewers, who'd do something like that?" Nelly wondered, bringing her coffee cup to her mouth, her little finger extended – she was a real lady. "Who would throw diamonds away?"

"There was a man on the phone. He said they belonged to him. A foreigner."

Nelly took a drink, knitting her brows, the coffee was too hot. Her features were getting more sharply defined, her shoulders skinnier, her bosom flatter. She's unhappy, Erika thought, she's alone too much.

"A foreigner?" Nelly asked. "Could it be a gangster perhaps?"

Erika looked out across the snow. There was a blackbird standing there, a black bird on a white expanse.

"I've no idea what kind of man it was, but what I am sure of is that he knows that Erdogan has found the diamonds. And I'm just as sure that he wants them back."

'You don't say." Nelly's voice was quivering with excitement. "It's just like a film. If I were you I'd keep my eye on him to make sure he doesn't clear off with them. If he does, you won't see him again."

"I am keeping my eye on him. I want him to stay here and I don't want anything to happen to him."

"These crazy things keep happening to you," Nelly said. "Nothing happens to me. I just sit there at home wasting away. I'm even glad when you call and ask if I can take your shift. To be honest, I miss you."

She smoothed down her blouse with her long, thin, sad fingers, the nails painted purple.

"Once this business is over, we'll head off to Greece together," Erika promised. "At the moment it's just not possible. Sometime later. Sorry."

She looked out across the expanse of snow, at the row of houses across the forecourt, at the overcast sky above.

"I've booked for Cyprus," Nelly told her, "a week's walking holiday in the Troodos mountains. You can go skiing there in the winter. But it's probably not much fun alone."

The blackbird had gone, the fine imprints of its claws could be seen.

"By the way," Erika asked, "can I come and stay with you for a few days if things get dicey?"

Nelly nodded. "Any time, for as long as you like. You know that."

Peter Hunkeler was sitting in his office staring at a sheet of paper and thinking. It was just after two, his stomach was full and he had difficulty concentrating. He'd had lunch in the Art Gallery restaurant, the dish of the day: veal stew, noodles and salad. He'd talked to people he'd known for years, two men in advertising and a retired doctor. They'd discussed the town's football club, whether they would be promoted back into the top league or not. After all, Basel was the second-largest city in Switzerland and it was scandalous that they had no club in the top league. The topic kept going throughout their lunch. One of the advertising men, who had clearly been a good footballer in his younger years, tended to work himself up into a fury – as if in a game of jass he'd just played the second-highest trump and his partner had over-trumped it.

Hunkeler hadn't contributed much to the discussion. He couldn't care less about FC Basel. He'd just listened and that had calmed him down.

Now he took up his ballpoint and noted:

1) Kayat intended to give the diamonds to Huber at Badischer Station, but was interrupted and flushed them down the toilet. Madörin is checking.

2) The intended recipient of the diamonds is unknown.

3) Kayat disappeared from the Drei Könige Hotel. Schneeberger and Lüdi are looking for him.

4) There was a break-in at the sewage workers' changing room. It could have been Kayat looking for the diamonds.

5) It is more than possible that diamonds flushed down the toilet could be found by the sewage workers. Overlapping.

6) At the time in question, a sewage worker by the name of Erdogan Civil was clearing the connection from Badischer

Station, which was blocked. It is possible that he found the diamonds then.

7) A man called one of the sewage workers this morning and asked about diamonds. It could be that that was Kayat who had found the names in the changing room.

8) If Civil has found the diamonds, it is possible that Kayat will find out sooner or later. Perhaps he already knows, in which case Civil is in danger.

9) That leaves the question of for whom the diamonds were ultimately intended. A clue could be Huber. Huber lives in a house in Gempenfluhstrasse that belongs to Infex. He works for that firm. Infex belongs to Dr Zeugin.

10) It's quite a crazy story.

11) Conclusion: Shadow Erdogan Civil, as unobtrusively as possible so as not to warn off someone (e.g. Kayat) who may be following him. Haller to do that. Look for Kayat (Lüdi and Schneeberger). Question Dr Zeugin.

Hunkeler lit a cigarette. He simply needed one, it helped him to think better.

The door opened, Madörin came in, seething with rage. Without a word he slurped the coffee he'd brought.

"Had a nice shower?" Hunkeler asked.

Madörin tried to smile but was only half-successful. "The next time it's you going down there, that's for sure."

"So? Did you find anything?"

"No. Just shit and rats." He tossed the empty cup into the trash.

"Well done," said Hunkeler. "Now tell me everything."

Madörin closed his eyes, he seemed to be thinking. "If the stones were down there, then that Turk's already got them. Or do you see that differently?"

112

Hunkeler shrugged.

"And that I was made to go down there was sheer bloody-mindedness on your part."

"Nonsense. How many access points are there?"

"There's no direct access to the sewers from the station. But there are three covered drains that run into them. All three were covered in snow, untouched. No one had been down there before us."

"That was something I'd also assumed. Kayat is a gentleman. He won't get his suit dirty."

"And what about me?" By now Madörin was really furious. "Am I not a gentleman?"

"You're a policeman."

Madörin got up and went out, slamming the door behind him.

Hunkeler stubbed out his cigarette, picked up the telephone directory, found the number of Infex and dialled it. He was nervous. He'd rather go down the shit pipe than call Dr Zeugin.

A woman's voice replied, friendly and good-humoured. "Infex. Yes?"

"May I speak to Dr Zeugin?"

"Who shall I say is calling?" she trilled.

"Inspector Hunkeler," he said in as friendly a way as he could manage but it was still more of a growl than a trill. "Basel police."

For a moment there was no sound, then the voice was back and not at all friendly now. "One moment, please."

Hunkeler was drumming the fingers of his left hand on the table. He was good at that, as a child he'd spent hours drumming on tables, with the fingertips of both hands on

113

the wood. He loved it, and there were kinds of wood on which it sounded really good.

"Yes, Zeugin here," came a sonorous male voice. "What is it?"

Hunkeler's hand had calmed down again. "I would like a word, if you are free."

"About what?"

"About Anton Huber. He lives in one of the houses that belong to you. The day before yesterday we arrested him at Badischer Station, took him in to the Lohnhof and then released him."

"I know," Dr Zeugin said, coolly and quietly, "he told me. A load of nonsense."

"What is his connection to you?"

"He works for me – as a driver. He drives international transport trucks, mainly to Portugal. A very reliable employee. Is that enough for you?"

Hunkeler's fingers started their drumming again in a quiet drum-roll for him alone.

"I would very much like to know what he was doing at Badischer Station and what his relationship with Guy Kayat is."

"Guy Kayat?" The voice held pure astonishment. "Never heard of him. Who is that?"

"'That' is a Lebanese citizen who we have every reason to believe is a courier of the profits from drugs. He's been on our database for some time."

"And what has that got to do with Anton Huber?"

"We have every good reason to suspect that this Kayat was bringing diamonds worth well over a million francs to Basel in order to hand them over to Huber."

There was a deep intake of breath, followed by another, then Zeugin's voice again, hard as nails. "Bizarre. Very bizarre this story you're telling me. And on what is this strange suspicion based, if I might ask?"

Hunkeler kept his calm. "We had a tip."

"A tip was it? And might I ask where this tip came from?"

"Of course you may ask, that goes without saying," Hunkeler said in his sweetest voice, "but unfortunately I'm not allowed to tell you. Surely you must understand that. We can't betray our sources, can we?"

"Of course you can't, of course," Dr Zeugin said. "Naturally you have to keep your channels open." A pause. "Yesterday afternoon Herr Huber went to collect an Egyptian businessman from Badischer Station. We import Egyptian cigarettes through him. Quite legally, of course. Unfortunately the businessman was unable to come to Basel that day. He didn't arrive until yesterday. He happens to be here in my office at the moment. Do you want to speak to him?"

"That won't be necessary," Hunkeler said. "Naturally I believe you."

"I hope you're not making some insinuation."

"An insinuation about what?" Hunkeler asked, as artlessly as a little child.

"Just you listen, you little police fellow." Dr Zeugin had had enough. He was leading three–nil, the game was over. "Don't you think you're going a little over the top? I'll tell you how it was – purely out of politeness. My employee Herr Huber had been instructed to collect my Egyptian business partner. Who didn't arrive. However, since it so happened that another well-dressed Arab arrived on the same train, Herr Huber went over to him to see whether it was the expected Egyptian. It wasn't. It was a simple misunderstanding. And Herr Huber would have been very happy to tell you that himself, if you had questioned him in a decent way. And incidentally, I can tell you, you little police fellow, that I think it is absolutely outrageous for you to descend on innocent citizens and arrest them. And I promise you that I'll be making a complaint. You'll be hearing from me. And the next time you want to speak to me be so good as to send me a summons. If you can manage that."

Clunk. End of message. The receiver had been replaced. And after a while came the comforting hum of the dialling tone.

Hunkeler was in definite need of a coffee, something warm and sweet, something full-bodied, strong, something to put new life into him now that he was feeling half-dead. But only half. The other half of him was already brightening up.

He went out into the corridor, pressed the third button on the machine and watched the coffee run down into the paper cup. He could smell the aroma, it brought a spark of hope. At least it smelt of coffee, even if it tasted like dishwater.

Suter, the public prosecutor, was coming up the stairs. "What's this I hear? That Kayat's disappeared?"

"That's right." Hunkeler took a sip. It did indeed taste like dishwater.

"Really?" Suter said, exasperated. "How is that possible? Are the Basel police not even capable of keeping watch overnight on a man in a hotel room?"

Hunkeler looked at him, not saying a word. Then he drank the rest of his coffee and dumped the cup in the wastepaper basket.

"It's your responsibility, Inspector. Just you remember that now," Suter shouted, so loud that a door opened further down and Madörin came out.

Hunkeler turned away, went into his office, sat down at his desk and wrote on the sheet of paper:

12) Dr Zeugin wants to know where we got the tip.

Guy Kayat was lying on his bed in the Hotel Rochat, asleep and fully dressed. It was two-thirty on a February afternoon. It was overcast, the temperature had risen and the snow was starting to thaw.

Kayat lay there calmly, like a tree. He was dreaming of Cyprus, of Nicosia, of the old town. That was where he lived but, in his dream, he suddenly couldn't find his way. Where there'd been a passageway there was now a wall, and where there'd been a wall there were steps leading up to an alleyway. Kayat went up, quite quickly. There was not a soul to be seen, it was a strange twilight, and suddenly he knew he was being followed. He ran, he could hear the over-loud slap of his leather soles on the pavement. He came out in a circular place completely enclosed by small houses, there was no gap between them. They seemed unoccupied. They seemed to be waiting for him, for the clatter of his soles, for his voice, his breath. But something told him it was a trap. If he were to push open a door and go in, it would close behind him and he'd be caught.

Kayat was standing in the middle of the houses, helpless, breathless. He could sense his pursuers approaching, but he couldn't hear them, they were moving silently. He went over to a door, pushed it and it gave way. In front of him was a dark corridor. He had no choice, he went along the corridor and after a few steps heard the door closing behind him.

He was lying on his back, he was fully dressed, he'd been dreaming in broad daylight. The window was open a crack. Organ music could be heard from outside.

Kayat got up and looked out. Facing him was the side of a church with Gothic windows and a steep roof from which the snow had fallen into the street. There was someone playing the organ in the church, always the same run of notes, five up, three down, with a brief trill in between that was clearly causing the organist difficulties.

He felt feverish, but that was normal. He often experienced that on his journeys, when he flew from warm regions to cold ones, or from cold to warm. He would be overtaken by this same weariness in his limbs. And anyway, he'd hardly slept at all in the last two nights. The diamonds. Those bloody stones. Because of them he'd had to take a laxative, climb down a wall on a snowy night and break into a changing room. And now he had a new name as well.

He was on the run. That was presumably why he'd had that dream of being trapped with the door closing. But he could only flee the country after he'd found the diamonds and handed them over to the man who was employing him.

He was in a real fix.

At least there was one lead he could follow up – the Turk. He would pay him a visit that evening.

The organist started to play with great gusto, drawing full, resounding chords from the pipes.

Kayat felt as if he was locked up in that small room. He slipped into his shoes and put on his camel-hair coat. Down in the foyer he handed in his key with a polite smile.

Outside he hesitated. What was he actually going to do, what was he looking for? Across the street in front of him was a square sparsely planted with trees, a grove. There were crows perched up in them, not making a sound. Some snow fell down from one of the branches, landing on the ground with a dull thud, and the branch whipped back up. The organist in the church was practising runs again, this time without repeats, however. He fingered the notes into the pipes one after the other with precision, like a string of pearls.

He went over to the monument outside the church, a bust on a plinth, covered in snow. The man was called Johann Peter Hebel, according to the inscription. He'd never heard of him.

He walked past the church and came out in a wide lane. The old houses looked as if they'd grown there. Snow was spilling over the gutters and threatening to fall.

Further along he turned left into Imbergässlein. For a moment he thought about his dream. Strange: in that he'd been going up, here he was going down.

He took the steps slowly and carefully. They were covered in ice, dull watery ice, no longer transparent and crisp, but still slippery. Some of the houses appeared to be unoccupied, their shutters were closed.

There was no one at all in the lane. He suddenly had problems with the steps. It wasn't that he had lost the strength to keep himself on his feet, you didn't need strength to go down. It was something else, something in his knees, in his back, inside his head. He realized that his whole body had grown tense and was covered with sweat. He stopped, rested both hands against the wall and tried to lower his head and relax his neck.

He had experienced this before. He was in the grip of stress, the urge to run away, which he mustn't give in to, the fear that stiffened him. He started to retch, the feeling came from deep down inside and was rising uncontrollably. It was shaking his body like the shivers. Then he started coughing, coughing until the tears came to his eyes, until he was vomiting. It wasn't proper vomiting, despite the torment – he noted that quite coolly. There was nothing in his stomach to bring up, he hadn't eaten yet, immediately after the calls in the early morning he had fallen back into a deep sleep.

Then the coughing stopped, as if his energy was drained. Kayat stayed leaning against the wall for a moment. Bending down, he picked up a handful of snow and pressed it to his face. Water ran down into his mouth, icy cold.

He dropped the snow, dried his face with his handkerchief, combed his hair. Pathetic, the way he was standing there in the lane, shaking with fear, panic-stricken. And that dream of the steps and the square with no exit was a load of nonsense.

He took a cigarette out of the packet, lit it and took a deep drag. He felt completely OK again. It had been a fit of nerves, nothing else, hunger perhaps. He desperately needed something to eat.

He went up the rest of the steps to Schneidergasse. There was a bar-restaurant on the left, a ventilator was whirling out smoky air. Over the door it said Château Lapin.

Kayat went in and sat at the long wooden table on the left. The place was half-full. In one corner were middle-aged women with weatherbeaten faces in thick woollen cardigans, clearly market women. They had glasses of light-coloured coffee in front of them. There were men with alcoholic drinks, old and young, some with beards, others bald, a few sitting at the table by the bar. No one looked up, no one seemed bothered by the foreign-looking man. There was an oil heater in the middle of the room, the soft flicker of its flame could be heard.

Kayat felt happy there. He gave his order to the waitress, a young woman with strong biceps and bright, lively eyes: tea with lemon but no milk and something to eat. There was spaghetti with mince, rösti with ox liver and ox-cheek salad. He chose the spaghetti.

When he got back to the Hotel Rochat a good hour later, a lady in a short leopard-skin coat was sitting in the lobby. She looked up at him with a delightful smile. "Herr Assad Harif?"

She stood up, long-legged as a gazelle. He shot a brief look at her fishnet stockings, which seemed to please her.

"I have an important message for you. May I accompany you up to your room?"

Kayat nodded, collected his key from the porter and they went up the stairs together.

"My name is Fränzi Fornerod," she said, once he'd closed the door behind him.

"Pleased to meet you. Please sit down. My name is…"

"I know," she said. "You are Monsieur Harif from Syria, aren't you?"

"As you say," he said with a slight bow.

121

She looked round. Her smile was gone. She clearly didn't feel happy there. "Cramped, isn't it, not like the Drei Könige?"

He said nothing, just shrugged.

"Right then." Now she was speaking in a cool, matter-of-fact voice, the charm gone. "I'm to take you to my apartment, the boss says. A few things have happened that make it impossible for you to stay in a hotel any longer. I have a two-room apartment in Hegenheimerstrasse. You can have one of the rooms until the matter is settled. He's waiting for the stones is the message I'm to give you from him. You understand?"

Kayat nodded.

"Right then. We're to drive straight to my apartment without wasting any time, the boss says. I've been waiting down below for half an hour, so get your things packed and come with me."

Kayat didn't say a word. He picked up his bag, opened the door, let her go out first and locked the room. He watched her as she walked along the corridor in front of him in her high heels, and suddenly there was a gentle swing to her hips.

Once more Erdogan Civil was the last man in the showers. He didn't know why it was always like that. He simply had slower hand movements than his colleagues, washed himself more thoroughly or liked the water running down over his body better.

That evening it was intentional. He scrubbed his bald patch and thinning hair as if he had to wash away a month-old crust of dirt, he kept rinsing it, letting the water pour down over him. Now and then he looked across into the changing room where his colleagues were getting dressed and the two workmen who had repaired the locks were packing up their tools. Their new keys were lying there on the bench.

Berger was the last to leave. "Make sure you lock up properly," he said. "See you tomorrow."

Erdogan waited a while until he was sure he was alone. He dried himself, first his head then his shoulders, back and belly, finally his toes. He saw to them with tender loving care, suddenly they seemed beautiful to him. He gave a brief grin – of pleasure, of pride – for he'd hoodwinked them all, his colleagues, the foreman, the police. The only opponent left was the foreign-sounding man who'd rung that morning. But he would put one over on him too, he was at least as crafty as him.

He got dressed and peeped out to see if the coast was clear. Then he walked briskly, taking care not to run, over to his moped, took the plastic bag off the luggage rack and went back into the changing room. He put the bag at the bottom of his locker under a pullover, then locked it. He also locked the changing room door, then got on his moped and headed off through the post-work traffic for Dreirosenbrücke. There was still snow on the road but it wasn't frozen anymore.

On the bridge there was the usual traffic jam. He squeezed his way through on the right of the delivery trucks. A few times he was forced into the heap of snow in the gutter, but he never fell off. He felt strong on his moped. Like a wild, bold rider, like Memed the Hawk.

123

He stopped outside Café Ankara on Colmarerstrasse. As he slowly took off his helmet, he checked out the surrounding area. A few cars went past, everything was normal.

In the cafe window there was a board with charter flights to Turkey. The next flight was to Izmir in three days' time: 11.30 on Saturday morning from Zurich-Kloten.

Erdogan went into the cafe and sat down at one of the tables where some men were playing cards. Some of them gave him a nod then concentrated on the game again. He was known there but he hadn't been a regular since he'd been living with Erika. He'd been fortunate and he deserved it.

Muhammed Ali brought him his tea. "Everything OK?" he asked.

Erdogan nodded, "Yes, everything's OK. By the way, I'm going to Turkey on Saturday. Is there still a seat left on the flight to Izmir?"

"One moment." Muhammed Ali went behind the bar and tapped away on a computer. "Reserved," he said when he came back to the table. "You can pick up the ticket here on Friday evening. How's Erika?"

"Everything's fine with Erika. And at home in Selçuk everything's fine as well."

"We rarely see you," Muhammed Ali said. "You're still in love?"

Erdogan laughed, picked up the glass and sipped the hot tea.

"OK," Muhammed Ali said, "see you Friday evening."

It was gone seven when Erdogan turned into Lörracherstrasse. The streets were empty. There was nothing suspicious, no movement, everything was quiet. He put the moped away in the bicycle park, took off his helmet and had another good look round again.

Right outside next door there was a man sitting in a car studying a street map. He didn't look up, quietly drawing on his curved pipe and puffing out the smoke.

It worried Erdogan. Gathering up his courage he took a closer look. That was a respectable man there in the car, a Swiss, a quiet pipe-smoker looking for an address on the street map of the city. He definitely wasn't a criminal.

Diagonally opposite was the American car. It was too conspicuous, it showed his wealth, it had to go.

Reaching a decision, Erdogan crossed the road and began to wipe the snow off the roof. Once he'd scraped the windows clear he got in and turned on the ignition. After some spluttering the engine started. He had already put it into first gear when in the rear-view mirror he saw a car approaching. It was a small red car with four-wheel drive and an aerial. Erdogan waited for the other car to pass, but it stopped alongside him. The man at the wheel smiled and gave a wave. And despite the darkness it was clear he was a foreigner, an Arab.

Erdogan sat there, rigid. Spellbound he watched the other car set off again, disappearing at the crossroads. Then he looked across at the pipe-smoker. He was still studying the street map, he hadn't noticed anything.

Erdogan changed back into neutral and left the engine on. There was nothing unusual about that, the engine had to warm up first.

Perhaps the Arab was the man who'd rung that morning. Perhaps, but it wasn't certain. If it was him, then the man would now know that he had an American car, a luxury motor. That meant: poor Turkish guest worker finds diamonds in the shit-pipe and the first thing he does is buy a swanky luxury limousine.

If only he'd listened to Erika and not bought the car. How was he going to get rid of it now?

He glanced across at the pipe-smoker again, to see if he'd noticed anything. He hadn't. Clearly he'd found the street he was looking for. He started the engine, switched on the lights and drove off.

Erdogan decided to park the car elsewhere and not to touch it for a while.

He set off and drove slowly over the crossroads. There was no sign of the foreigner's car, nor of the pipe-smoker's. Perhaps it had all been a false alarm. Perhaps it was just his nerves and he was seeing ghosts.

He parked the car on a dark stretch of Hammerstrasse, well away from the nearest street light. He locked all the doors and the trunk, then walked home.

Peter Hunkeler climbed the stairs to Erika's apartment. He loved these old staircases that smelled of dust and floor polish. The iron banisters with the worn handrails. The milk-glass globe lamps with their forty-watt bulbs. The holes in the plastered walls caused by unwieldy pieces of furniture.

It was almost entirely foreigners who lived here. He'd seen that from the names on the letterboxes down in the hall. Guest workers who did the dirty jobs in Switzerland and were happy to find cheap lodgings. It surprised him that Frau Waldis lived here. He would have expected a woman working at the checkout to be living in a one-room apartment in a newly built block with a lift and a small balcony. Nonsense, he told himself, always the same old stupid prejudices.

He wiped his shoes clean on the mat outside Erika's door, more out of embarrassment than necessity. There was something scraping on the floor, but he ignored it and rang the bell. The door opened and he went in.

Frau Waldis was a plump woman with long, dark-blond hair. She looked him over suspiciously. She was afraid, Hunkeler could see that clearly. And he could see just as clearly how well she concealed her fear.

He showed her his identification. She invited him to sit down. Erdogan wasn't in, she said, but he'd be back soon.

On a low table sat a teapot, along with a loaf, the remains of a liver sausage, slices of cold meat, some processed cheese and chopped onion.

She was just having a snack, she said, would he like to join her?

Thank you, but no, he said, though he had nothing against a drop of tea.

She fetched a cup from the kitchen and poured the tea. It wasn't your ordinary tea, it was lapsang souchong. Then she looked at him, fixedly, without saying a word.

Hunkeler put a card with his telephone number on the table.

"There," he said, "that's my work number, you will almost always be able to contact me there. That's my home number and that there is the number of my car telephone. You will definitely find me on one of those numbers, twenty-four hours a day."

Erika chewed her food, slowly and thoroughly. She didn't seem to be enjoying it much. She thought for a while. "Why should I call you?"

"If your friend has found these diamonds – and that is what we're assuming – then he's in danger. We know that there's a man after those diamonds, a professional, and that means he'll be after Herr Civil as well. The man is working in the drugs trade and in the drugs trade they're absolutely ruthless. He'll find out sooner or later if Herr Civil actually has the diamonds – and, as I said, we're almost certain of that. Once he knows, he'll force Herr Civil to hand over the stones and, if Herr Civil refuses, he'll use force. That's the last moment when you can call me. Perhaps we'll be able to intervene then. It would be much better if you told us the truth now, though. That would certainly be the best solution."

"The best solution." She bit off a piece of cheese and spent some time chewing it. "Who can say what's best? Would you like more tea?"

Hunkeler nodded and she refilled his cup.

"I know nothing about any diamonds," she said looking him straight in the eye. If she's lying, he thought, then she's doing it very well.

"Have you not noticed anything unusual about your friend in the last few days?" he asked. "Nervousness, that kind of thing?"

"No." Again that clear, untroubled look.

"What about that toothache yesterday? Did he go to the dentist?"

"No. The toothache just went away."

"Oh, he was lucky then." He picked up his cup and took a sip. It really was particularly good lapsang souchong.

"Top back left," she said, "a molar. He has very bad teeth anyway. He ought to have had them seen to ages ago. But it's the money that's the problem. There's a whole family in Turkey that lives on his money. An extended family with uncles and aunts and great-aunts. They live on what a molar would cost here in Switzerland. He says you can live without a tooth but not without bread."

Hunkeler knew there was no point in saying any more. The lady wasn't for turning and that was that.

"Where does he live in Turkey?" he asked, just to change the subject.

"Selçuk. It's close to Izmir."

"I know," Hunkeler said. "It's near Ephesus. I spent a few days there in a new chalet hotel."

"You don't say." She looked at him in astonishment and suddenly seemed interested.

"There are flamingos there and any number of turtles," he told her. "I counted four species. And storks. In the evening they fly back to the nests they've built on the Roman viaduct in the middle of Selçuk. A paradise. It'll be ruined in the near future. They've built a dam right across the marshes by the sea. There are already street lamps out there on the beach, even though there's no road yet. But I'm sure you'll have been there already as well."

She'd listened, rapt. "No," she said, her expression suddenly weary. She picked up her plate and took it into the kitchen, came back with a tea cosy and put it over the pot. "I presume you haven't any objection if I watch the news?"

Hunkeler said he hadn't and she switched the TV on, just at the right moment. The newsreader listed the topics: Should Switzerland join the EEA? Should the state make heroin available for the worst addicts? War in Yugoslavia. And the weather: a warm front was coming.

Hunkeler sat on the low armchair with half an ear on the news. Everything had been said, but he intended to wait another half-hour for Civil.

He was enjoying sitting there. He liked the woman. There was a calmness about her that he found soothing. Strangely enough he didn't feel the least desire for a cigarette.

He looked across at the aquarium on the sideboard, at the goldfish motionless by a dark aquatic plant. Oxygen was bubbling up out of a little tube with a sound you hardly noticed, it was so regular. On the bottom there was black sand, about two inches deep, like fine coffee grounds – they ought really to have checked out the sand to see whether there was anything glittering and gleaming in it.

Erdogan arrived shortly before eight. He had a visible fright when he saw Hunkeler, but he quickly got a grip on himself. He'd just been to have a beer, he said, in a bar somewhere, he'd felt thirsty and when he was thirsty he usually had a drink.

Hunkeler had stood up and watched him take off his coat and hang it up, take the empty beer bottle out of the pocket and put it on the table, sit down and pour himself a cup of tea. He did all that calmly, as a matter of course. And in the same calm and matter-of-course way Frau Waldis cut two slices of bread for her man, spread butter on them, put some sliced cold sausage on the one and cheese on the other and pushed them over to him. He ate them, chewing slowly, gave a brief burp, then swallowed and waited.

Hunkeler was still standing there. It was obvious that he was in the way. Pointing to his card on the table, he said, "If you change your mind, then call me. As soon as possible. Please remember that the police are there to protect people. We are able to do that at any time. Don't think you can deal with those criminals on your own. Please trust me."

He felt a bit stupid saying all that, but it was honest. He felt he was a friend and helper to these two people.

"What's all that stupid stuff?" the little man said. "I can't understand a word."

"I was in Selçuk eighteen months ago," Hunkeler said, with no idea why he was saying it, perhaps he just wanted to gain time, "it was September and the sea was still warm. We had a place outside the town, on the beach, and every afternoon we drove into Selçuk. Once we went in a community taxi. It was coming from one of the villages on the edge of the marshes out there and it was crowded with people, young and old. Despite that they picked us up. There was a mood in that car I'll never forget. It was solemn, almost holy, if you see what I mean. I'll try to explain that. Even though it was just a trip to the nearest main town of the district, for those people it was a journey to a different continent. Their mood, the way they looked out of the car as it went along the dam across the marshes, was reverent. Reverence, yes, that's the right word. Can you understand what I'm saying?"

"The car was a dolmus," the little man said, "that's what they have down there."

"You don't understand," Hunkeler said. "I'll try to explain it in a different way. We hired a car and drove off into the hills and came to a lake. There was just one house by the lake, the fisherman's house. There was a boat on the shore. We stopped and went down to the water. It was full of life. Fish, frogs, crabs, newts, and then the birds: storks,

131

herons, ducks. It was nature unspoiled, just as in the days of Solomon. A beauty that was almost too much for me. Not far from that lake there was a village and there was a stork's nest on the roof of every house. We drove into the village square and were immediately surrounded by laughing, delighted men. They wanted us to get out and accept an invitation to stay there, at least for one night. I was at the wheel and I immediately turned round. I fled from that village. I was in flight from beauty. Now can you understand me?"

The little man had listened. He went on eating and seemed to be thinking, but he said nothing.

"That place where the world was still in order," Hunkeler went on, "the marsh with the flamingos, the lake with the storks, the community taxi with the reverent passengers, the village with the men who welcome a stranger as a king and want to entertain him as a king – all of that will be ruined in a few years' time. Do you understand me now?"

"Yes," the little man said. "I can understand what you say. But people are more important than turtles and flamingos. Hotels mean work. A road on an embankment across the marshes is built by men who earn money for that. Or should they and their families starve just because you like to see a stork in the sky now and then?"

"No, that shouldn't happen to them," Hunkeler said.

He watched Civil pick up one of the slices of bread, take a bite and chew.

"Diamonds are something wonderful," he said, "and I can well understand that someone who finds a handful won't want to give them up."

"Oh, stop going on about those diamonds. I haven't got any."

"Sorry to have disturbed you," Hunkeler said. "I wish you both a very good evening. And all the best."

He went out.

Peter Hunkeler sat in his car and switched on the engine. He was nervous, he wasn't happy with himself. Why had he gone on like that about storks and frogs, about beauty and an unspoiled world, what had he been trying to say? And then that nonsense about the destruction of the environment in Turkey, what was that to do with him? That false morality trying to forbid other people to do what had already happened here years ago. Wasn't it just a few years ago that every church roof here in Switzerland had a stork's nest stuck to it, where they'd laid their eggs and brought up their young? And what had happened with the Altachenbach, the stream by which he'd grown up? Where had the water lilies gone, the leeches and trout? They weren't there anymore, they'd disappeared.

It had just been the usual arrogant Swiss know-all attitude, a penchant for telling other people what to do, that had made him make that speech. He had been trying to make his sympathy clear to the man from Turkey, to show that he found him likeable, that he knew a bit about the country he came from, how beautiful it was, its unbelievable sense of hospitality. He was using that expression of sympathy to make the man trust him, and naturally he'd failed to get anywhere with it.

The man from Selçuk wasn't here on a pleasure trip because he thought Basel was a beautiful city of humanists.

He wasn't spending eight hours a day crawling round the drains because he particularly liked the smell of sewage – he did it because he wanted to earn money. A determined man, this Civil. He had clear views, he knew what he wanted. If he had actually found the diamonds, he'd do his utmost to keep them.

And Frau Waldis? Why had she not said anything? She hadn't said anything because she was afraid. She wasn't just afraid of strangers forcing their way into her apartment, she was above all afraid of losing her Erdogan. Hunkeler had seen how interested she'd been in his description of Selçuk and how weary she'd suddenly looked when he'd asked her whether she'd been there too.

She didn't want to see Erdogan disappear to Turkey, never to return.

But weren't the diamonds good reason for Civil to go back home a rich man? And if that was something she wanted to prevent, shouldn't she have spoken? She hadn't said anything because that would be a betrayal. And her love was something she wouldn't and couldn't betray.

Or was that all wrong? Did Civil really know nothing about the diamonds? At least the business with the toothache seemed to be genuine.

And where was Haller anyway? Surveillance of the Turk was his job. Was he having a break again?

Hunkeler switched the engine off and tapped out Haller's number on his telephone. He picked up after the first bleep.

"Where on earth are you?" Hunkeler asked.

"He saw me," Haller said, "so I quietly cleared off. I'm a hundred yards down towards the Rhine now. Can you see the petrol station?"

"Yes."

"I'm just past it. I've got the situation under control. By the way, the Turk's got a Yankee motor, a fantastic model, really great, white with a red top." You could hear him drawing on his pipe and blowing the smoke out.

"Well, well," Hunkeler said, "what a surprise. Keep at it, then."

He put the phone down, started the engine and drove off. So Civil had a Yankee motor. And when had he bought that? Perhaps yesterday when he hadn't been at work because of toothache at the back, top left?

Hunkeler turned into Rheingasse and parked right next to the taxi rank where there was no parking. He stuck his ID card under the nose of the taxi driver who'd got out and was coming to tell him to clear off. The man gave a military salute.

There wasn't much traffic on the road, it was still too early. Or perhaps the boozers of both sexes had used the snow as an excuse to stay at home and get pickled by their own stoves.

Only the druggies were there. They – junkies and dealers – were standing on the right in the underpass that went down to the Rhine. One was sitting on the ground, the needle stuck in his arm, doubled over, the picture of extreme concentration. Others were squatting there beside him, smoking. Someone set a tape recorder playing. On the left, twenty yards further on, concealed by some scaffolding, was Detective Sergeant Madörin, a walkie-talkie in his hand. He was staring fixedly, observing something on the other side. There on the pavement opposite, right next to the entrance to the Swiss Chalet, a popular dance hall with

Swiss folk music, a young woman was sitting in the snow, legs stretched out, her back against the wall of the building. A young man was kneeling beside her, shaking her, slapping her face; then he stopped and looked for help from the taxis waiting there.

Hunkeler got out. That image of the young woman with the long black hair, he recognized it – yet it couldn't be, mustn't be. But for a brief moment he was sure it was his daughter Isabelle sitting against that wall.

He went over, not quickly but slowly, checking it out. He felt like dashing across, pulling his daughter up and holding her in his arms, but the feeling of horror held him back. He saw that for a moment the young man was about to run off, but then he stayed. Hunkeler bent down over the woman, whose hair covered her face. He cautiously drew the hair aside, saw that he was looking at an unknown face.

It wasn't Isabelle.

The woman was breathing slowly, far too slowly. In the light of the street lamp her face had a bluish shimmer.

"Overdose," the young man said. "She's my girlfriend. Can you help?"

Hunkeler nodded. He went across to Madörin, tore the telephone out of his hand and called for an ambulance. Then he went back over to the woman. "Hold her tight," he said, "keep her warm. Slap her across the face, but not too hard."

He took off his coat and the two of them wrapped her up in it as well as they could. Her red knitted scarf had slipped off and was lying in the snow. He rolled it up, watching the young man put his arms round his girlfriend and awkwardly slap her across the face with the back of his hand.

Madörin came across. "I thought she was asleep. Is it bad?"

"If she dies," Hunkeler said, "then you're for it for failure to offer assistance in an emergency. You can be sure of that."

Madörin grimaced and spat on the snow. "She's not going to die, they're tough, they are." He wasn't happy. He stood there like an unloved uncle. "It's not my fault if some woman drugs herself up to the eyeballs."

The ambulance was there in five minutes. Once the woman was in it Hunkeler said to the young man, "Go with her. Stay with her. And for God's sake keep a close eye on her in future."

Hunkeler drove over Wettsteinbrücke back into Greater Basel. He had to talk to someone now, anyone, friends or just acquaintances. He needed the society of normal human beings.

If the stuff were distributed in a controlled way by the state, then these accidents wouldn't happen. But people clearly didn't care about that. The odd heroin corpse had no impact on the public sense of justice, it wasn't their fault.

But then what would Hunkeler have done if the young woman back there in the snow had been his own daughter? Would he have been able to carry on his normal round from bed to the office, from the office to lunch, from lunch back into the office, and from the office to the bar for an evening beer, as if nothing had happened? Would he have been able to quietly continue stoking up the stove and crawling into bed with Hedwig just before midnight with the same sense of well-being?

No, he wouldn't have been able to do that any longer. He would have been marked by that picture of wretchedness to the end of his life.

For a brief moment Hunkeler felt like saying a short prayer as he drove over the bridge; something like: "For what we are about to receive may the Lord make us truly thankful" – only with a different meaning. And, without intending to, he said loud and clear: "Dear God, help my daughter Isabelle."

A strong wind caught his car, pushing it out into the middle of the road. It was from the west, the wind had turned. It was now coming from the Atlantic, across the plains of France, bringing warm, wet weather.

Hunkeler parked outside the Art Gallery and went in. As it was every evening, the restaurant was full. On the right were the tables with white cloths where you had the à la carte menu. Elderly couples were sitting there with a bottle of wine, exchanging an occasional quiet word, the discreet ladies smartly dressed, hoping for an adventure that never materialized. There were a few gay couples, hair close-cropped, paying no attention to their surroundings, gazing at each other adoringly. Then the female couples – Hunkeler could never tell whether they were lesbians – one telling a lengthy story, the other listening. In the middle of the room was a table with a five-foot-high flower arrangement that immersed the surrounding company in a blaze of colour and fragrance. On the wall at the back was a picture of people playing boccia, painted by Paul Camenisch, a gay communist who died an old man in 1970, hated and ostracized by the bourgeois set that now found his pictures beautiful.

Two tables had been pushed together below the picture and an illustrious group of men were gathered there. Hunkeler knew them all. Two directors of Basel Chemie; a former advertising executive who had sold his company and didn't know what to do with so much money; an architect from one of the leading families in the city, formerly a member of parliament and still an enthusiastic participant in the delights of the Shrovetide carnival, an excellent pen-and-ink artist in his free time. Then there was Hunkeler's boss, the police commissioner, another man with wide-ranging cultural interests and talents; he not only enjoyed the brass of the Basel Police Band but also the delicate stroke on a violin.

It was the Culture for Basel committee, which was sponsoring and organizing "World in Song" week. And among them were Suter, the state prosecutor, and Dr Zeugin, formerly a fiduciary agent, now an importer.

Hunkeler had merely glanced at the group then immediately slipped off to the left, into the other part of the Gallery, generally known as the Tube. At the moment he didn't want to be seen by those gentlemen, he was still furious. They were sitting there, with the best of intentions, talking about shepherd choirs in the Caucasus, the call to the herd of the Tuareg in the Hoggar Mountains, and yodelling pygmies. And all the while young people were dying on the streets of Basel because they had nowhere to meet, no indoor space, no money. Because these elderly gentlemen were the ones who decided what culture was.

It was almost entirely young people in the Tube. Harmless, lively youngsters, good-looking, closely packed, hip to hip. At least there's that, Hunkeler thought, at least in this place they're all sitting together under the one roof, the powerful and the powerless, even if they don't talk to each other.

He crossed the room and went to sit at a table on the right at the back, where some men of his own age were sitting. The two advertising men from lunchtime were there and the pastor from the nearby church, a shy, melancholy brooder. There was also an artist who'd enjoyed some success, his mouth full of bad teeth, lively curiosity and wit in his eyes. Finally the owner of the restaurant, an elegant man of Lombard grandeur whose immigrant grandfather had been a bricklayer.

Hunkeler usually felt happy at that table. People drank, but in moderation, they thumped the table as they made their point, they discussed problems that concerned everyone with a nod and a wink. And almost always there was harmony there.

But that evening things didn't work out that way. Hunkeler had worked himself up into too much of a rage.

"I've just seen a young woman lying in the snow in Rheingasse," he said, "with death written all over her face. And no one lifted a finger. Is that what's normal in this town now?"

He took a mouthful of the beer the waiter had put down in front of him. He didn't enjoy it. "For a moment I thought it was my daughter."

"Oh do stop moaning," the artist said, "or go and tell the gentlemen over there. It's their responsibility."

"There's a man I know," the older of the two advertising men said, "who has emphysema. It comes from smoking. Despite that he's still smoking. How can a drug addict give it up if even a harmless smoker can't?"

Lighting a cigarette himself, Hunkeler said, "We're old. But they're young. They're our children and I can't stand it when I have to watch them destroying themselves."

"Don't start going on about the whales and the Indians again," the artist said.

"Oh yes I will," Hunkeler said. "I'll start with them and finish with our children."

"That's enough of that nonsense," the other advertising man said. "Look after yourself a bit better before you go down the drain."

He waved the waiter over and told him to bring the cards, marker board and cloth for a game of jass. "Are you going to join in?"

"No," Hunkeler said.

He watched as the cards were brought and dealt and the men started to play. They picked up their cards and arranged them in one hand with intense concentration. You couldn't tell what any one of them was thinking.

He usually joined in these games if he was invited to. For him jass was one of the fine old traditions. But that evening he didn't feel like it.

"You're nothing but comfortable, gaga old arseholes, totally conformist," he said. He stood up, conscious of how they looked at him uncomprehending, as if he were sick.

"You're off your head," the owner said, "but it doesn't matter."

Hunkeler went out, got into his car, which had a parking ticket on the windshield, and drove off. He hated this town whose policeman he was. He hated these men, who were his friends. He hated himself.

This Dr Zeugin, who dealt in import and export via

all sorts of legitimate and shady channels, this man of honour who insisted on knowing where the Basel Criminal Investigation Department had got its tip about the dirty diamonds, this important, upstanding citizen was sitting at his table of honour with the other powers-that-be in this town, deciding what culture was. And why was he sitting there? Because he had money.

The old revolutionary had woken up inside Hunkeler. It wasn't the young people who saw a life ahead of them, an unknown, unformulated sweet life, who commanded the money, but the stale old fogeys with their pot bellies, with their lives behind them and nothing but death before them. Those impotent fuddy-duddies who couldn't manage a single erection anymore, not on their fortieth wedding anniversary, not on the first of May and not on New Year's Eve after a dozen oysters and a bottle of bubbly, which they slurped out of gold-rimmed crystal glasses. And that's precisely why they declare that people's money is untouchable and sacred, precisely why they sit there on their dough, because with it they can hang on to the power, which in the natural course of things they ought to have given up long ago, letting it accumulate until they are in the grave. They fuck with money and they fuck the younger generation.

Hunkeler groaned. Out of annoyance, out of fury, out of frustration with his wretched job, he couldn't say which. Power to the imagination, huh! He gave a bitter grin. Power to the moneybags, to the conformists, the squeaky-clean brigade with their shitty underpants! That was the way things really were.

He'd got so worked up that he almost drove into a car that had stopped in front of him at a red light. The snow on the street was thick and wet now, and the road was covered with slush.

He parked outside his apartment and walked the few steps from there to the Sommereck. Edi was there, as was Beat and a new man called André who looked like a life insurance salesman. Hunkeler ordered toasted cheese with an egg and white coffee. He said nothing, just listened and ate. Now and then he heard the music from the juke-box: "Buona sera, signorina, buona sera", "See you later alligator", the old evergreens and hits that had been his comfort when he was young, "Working for the Yankee dollar, yeah".

When, around eleven, Edi came over with the grappa bottle, Hunkeler waved it away. He didn't want any, he didn't feel like it. Yes, he wanted to sit there and listen. But boozing and talking were something he didn't want.

"A free delivery of grappa," Beat, the secondhand book-seller, said as Edi poured some. "That's a free delivery of drugs, and on premises open to the public to boot. Isn't that forbidden?"

The men shook with laughter, emptied their glasses and held them out for a refill.

"Now those over there are actually talking about whether the state should supply the stuff to the druggies for free. Have you heard that?" the newcomer asked. He was wearing a silver tiepin with a red jewel.

"That wouldn't be the most stupid thing to do," said Edi. "Why not, actually?"

André slammed his glass back down on the table. "Where do you think we're living? In a state self-service store? They should all be locked up and made to live on bread and water

143

until they're not addicted anymore or, as far as I care, give up the ghost. And the asylum seekers as well. Lock them up on bread and water till they see sense. Do you really think I want to see my taxes used to pay for their drugs, eh?"

Edi leaned back. He was for peace, didn't want to quarrel.

"You're a commercial traveller?" Hunkeler asked.

'Yes," André snarled. "Why do you ask?"

"Calm down," Edi said, "this man's a policeman."

"Oh really, the gentleman's a policeman," the man with the tiepin said nastily, and it was clear he'd had more than enough, a litre of alcohol, two litres of frustration and rage.

"The gentleman thinks it's beneath him to talk to simple citizens who work and pay their tax regularly. D'you know what I'd do if I were in power? Put them all up against the wall, druggies and asylum seekers, then let them have it with a machine gun, ratatattat."

Hunkeler stood up so quickly his chair fell over behind him. Stretching his arms over the table, he grabbed the man by the throat and throttled him for two, three seconds, then let go of him.

Edi leaped to his feet and grabbed him by the arm. "Calm down," he shouted, "have you gone mad?"

Still standing at the table, Hunkeler dropped his arms and looked across at André, who was sitting in his chair and staring at him, white as a sheet.

"Sorry," he said. "I'll pay tomorrow."

Outside a warm wind was blowing. It was more of a storm, a March storm. Hunkeler heard the snow on the roof behind him slide down onto the pavement.

What was wrong with him? Why had he suddenly wanted to throttle a man he didn't know at all?

144

He needed some sleep. He went to his apartment, set the alarm clock for seven and got into bed.

During the night the warm air that had been forecast swept over Basel. It rattled the shutters and carried the smoke away from the chimneys. It penetrated and melted the snow, it cleared the roofs. It blew the sleeping Baselers into their dreams.

In a few hours the Atlantic wind ate the snow away from the slopes and peaks of the surrounding mountains, and, since the ground was still frozen and couldn't absorb any water, it cascaded down into the valleys. At Zell the River Wiese burst its banks, blocking the road along the valley; at the embankment in Basel it overflowed onto the motorway approach road. The Birsig flooded the Heuwaage district, pouring down Steinenvorstadt across Barfüsserplatz and Marktplatz to the landing stage, where it joined the Rhine. Even the Birs overflowed its broad banks, suddenly turning into a wild torrent with powerful waves.

The Rhine rose to a level higher than it had been for decades, flooding the water meadows below the town. Huge trees, torn out of the slopes of the Jura, floated down to the Rhine dam and the locks at Kembs, turning and swirling.

At eight that Thursday morning, Inspector Hunkeler woke from a deep sleep. He looked at the alarm clock on the bedside table that was set for seven. Clearly it had rung, the button was up. But Hunkeler hadn't heard anything.

He got out of bed, put on some water for tea, washed, shaved and cleaned his teeth – the usual morning ritual.

Generally he found that tedious: all the scrubbing, scrap-ing, brushing and gargling. He felt it was pointless, the first step in the daily slavery he had chosen of his own free will.

On that morning he did all this with care, with love of himself, so it seemed. And he dabbed his clean-shaven chin with the outrageously expensive Eau des Lilas Hedwig had brought back from Paris for him.

He felt good. And he had no idea why. It wasn't just the fact that he'd had a long sleep. Perhaps it was that he'd managed not to hear the alarm clock for once and had slept for an extra hour. So he still wasn't a machine, he could still look forward to some human fallibility.

What's more, he'd got everything off his chest again, without thinking, without rhyme or reason, and had moved beyond that morning-after feeling of shame, of self-abasement, of the most grovelling apology by telephone. He knew that it was better to hand out swear words and, if there was any doubt, to let fly at some feeble-minded arsehole rather than keep everything bottled up inside. Smash whatever you can smash – he'd made that slogan his own. Speak your mind, speak your rage, get it out in the open or your anger will be bottled up inside you. But it wasn't something you could do every time. You got older, you quietened down, your canines wore away and fell out, leaving you sitting there, lips sucked in, saying nothing.

He drank three cups of tea standing up. As he went down the stairs he tried to whistle "Django" by the Modern Jazz Quartet. Beautiful soft notes.

He parked outside the Lohnhof.

In the office Schneeberger was sitting reading the newspaper. He looked up briefly, checked his watch and went on reading.

Hunkeler sat down, lit up and waited.

After a while Schneeberger said casually, "Haller called. Erdogan Civil went to work at two-thirty. Flood alert."

"And Kayat?"

"Oh yes, Kayat." Schneeberger kept him in suspense as he always did when he'd discovered something. "Kayat's got a new name. He's called Assad Harif now and is Syrian. He was in the Hotel Rochat until three yesterday afternoon and then went off. Where he's gone, we don't know."

"The Rochat? That's only five hundred yards from the Drei Könige."

"That's precisely why it took us so long to find him," Schneeberger said in schoolmasterly tones, "we'd assumed he'd move as far away as possible."

Hunkeler stood up, went over to the window and looked across at the maple tree. The three crows were perched there, a glossy black.

"That guy's leading us a merry dance," he said, "and I don't like that. Has he phoned anyone?"

Schneeberger shook his head in reproof. "Do you think he's stupid?"

"No."

"There's a telephone down in the lobby of the Rochat. He made several calls from there, at the crack of dawn."

Hunkeler nodded. That's what he'd assumed.

"When I was sitting in the lobby of the Drei Könige," Schneeberger said, "a taxi drew up on Tuesday afternoon, shortly before four, and a beautiful young woman got out.

147

She was wearing an imitation leopard-skin coat, which was rather short for this time of year but understandable – she had lovely legs."

"What kind of taxi was it?"

"I can't remember. What I do remember, on the other hand, is that she handed a yellow envelope to the uniformed hotel porter at the door."

"And?" Hunkeler asked.

"I'm telling you that because the person who collected Herr Kayat from the Rochat yesterday afternoon appears to have been a very beautiful young lady who was wearing a short, imitation leopard-skin coat. The hotel porter noticed that because of her lovely legs."

"What else did the porter notice?"

"Nothing, unfortunately. He has no idea what the two of them did when they went out, whether they got into a car or went off on foot."

Hunkeler went over to the table and gently stroked the beechwood surface. "And you didn't get the number of the taxi outside the Drei Könige?"

"I don't even know what firm it was. I can't make a note of everything."

"You did at least make a note of the coat and the legs. Well done."

Schneeberger swept that aside. "I've rung up every taxi firm in Basel and asked them to ask around to see who could have taken someone like that at the time in question. I bet the man will get back to me. You don't forget someone like that."

He stood up, crumpled the newspaper into a ball and threw it in the wastepaper basket.

Hunkeler turned to the window again. He watched the black birds in the tree, their strong beaks. Why were they perched here and not somewhere out in the woods?

He went to the door and turned the key. Then he sat down at the table, tipping the chair backwards and resting the soles of his feet on the edge of the desk. He put his arms round his knees, closed his eyes and waited. There was nothing he could think of to do. The opposition had the ball and now he just had to wait and hope they'd make some mistake. He mustn't miss it if they did, he had to be ready for that moment, that was all he could do.

He unlocked the door and went for a coffee. He relished it, even though it didn't taste any better than usual. But he was suddenly sure of the way things were going. This Kayat was on the run and they were on his tail. At some point or other he'd lose his nerve and, if they were lucky, he'd even lead them to his employer.

Hunkeler went down to the ground floor, where he fetched a camp bed and two blankets. He set it up by the window so that he could lie down and see the bare branches of the maple with the crows, which were still perched there, motionless. He locked the door again, loosened his tie, stretched out on the bed, wrapped one of the blankets round him and fell asleep.

He was woken by loud banging. Someone was knocking on the door.

He got up and opened it. It was Suter, puce with indignation.

"What are you thinking of, locking yourself in like that? You're isolating yourself. You're shirking your work, your responsibility, weirdo that you are. And what's this!?" he exclaimed when he saw the camp bed. "Is this what I think it is? You're sleeping off your drunkenness during working hours? At the state's expense? And how much did we drink again yesterday evening, Inspector, if I may ask?"

"You may," Hunkeler said. "I had a half litre of beer, but I didn't enjoy it. Then I had two cups of coffee with milk. I did enjoy those. After that I went to bed."

"That is outrageous, impertinent. You're simply mocking the state prosecution service. This isn't going to turn out well for you, my dear Inspector. This pigsty here has to be thoroughly cleared out. And I will make sure that happens – I myself."

Hunkeler sat down at the table. "I have a lead," he said, "made up of various parts that I can't quite put together at the moment. A kind of chain in which several links are missing. There's nothing I can do until further links appear, closing the gaps. So I can't do anything but wait. And that's what I'm doing here, in this room. And since this waiting looks as if it's going to last for several days I've taken the liberty of putting a bed in my office so that I can lie down and sleep on it. It so happens that I think best when I'm asleep, if that makes sense to you. I will wait here in this room until something happens. Even if it takes a week. I'm sure you don't want me to lie down on the cold floor and get a chill?"

"I couldn't care less about all this stuff about chains and links and trails," Suter shouted. "You've ruined the whole case. One hundred per cent. If the diamonds were actually down there in the sewers, then you should have gone and got them yesterday. Today it's too late. All the pipes are totally flooded. No poor devil's going to climb down there for you now, not a soul will go down. Don't you realize that?"

"The diamonds haven't been down there for ages."

"Oh. And where are they, then, if I may ask?"

"I've told you already – you may."

Suter was close to exploding, his face was so red. But he got himself under control, went to the window and took some deep breaths – a man who bore the responsibility but was under stress because of the incompetence of his subordinates. He turned round and said, "And why did you pester Herr Dr Zeugin, if I may ask?"

Aha, so that was the problem. Hunkeler inspected the fingernails of his left hand. He was going to have to cut them again, they just kept on growing.

"I was asking him about Herr Huber."

"I know. Huber is an employee of Dr Zeugin. What's suspicious about that?"

"I didn't tell Dr Zeugin there was anything suspicious about it, I simply chatted with him for a while."

"Oh, so that's what you call chatting, is it? Dr Zeugin was horrified. He's in shock. And quite rightly so. Dr Zeugin is a man of honour, absolutely, who does everything he can for this town. And now there's this nasty, insidious suspicion. I had to apologize for you, Inspector, and I felt deeply ashamed."

Suter had to sit down, so deeply was he ashamed.

"It's scandalous," he groaned, loosening his collar and scratching his neck in disappointment.

"I told Dr Zeugin that we'd had a hot tip about some dirty diamonds."

"Is there no end to it, to this wretched botched job?" Suter was close to tears.

"He appeared very interested to know from whom we'd

had the tip. He was actually insistent. I didn't tell him anything."

"What are you suggesting by that? If someone…"

"Nothing. I'm just saying that he seemed exceptionally interested in where the tip came from. I mean, it should be a matter of complete indifference to him."

Suter sat there, eyes down, for a long time. He seemed to be contemplating the wood of the desktop. Then he looked up, no longer so sure of himself.

"What you are suggesting here is monstrous. If that should happen to be true we'd have to call off our 'World in Song' project. It would be simply out of the question." He thought for a moment, his eyes closed, his lips twisted in an expression of suffering, almost embitterment. "Do you realize just how appalling your allegation is?"

"Yes," Hunkeler said. "We are both aware that the drugs business, which is worth millions, wouldn't be possible without the complicity of high-ups, would it, sir?"

Suter's eyes were fixed on a point far behind the wall he was staring at, far beyond any walls, miles away. "I know," he said quietly, almost too quietly to be heard. "The world is in an absolute mess. The devil's in command."

"So I'll carry on with my work," said Hunkeler, "shall I?"

"Do what you have to do, do your duty." Suter stood up. "You're stubborn as a mule. You're heading for disaster."

At midday Kayat woke from a dreamless sleep. He felt run-down, as if he'd been in bed for days recovering from a serious illness that had drained him of all his strength.

For a moment it was difficult for him to find his bearings in that wide-awake world and he wanted to return to the darkness. Then a heavy vehicle drove past outside, making the windowpanes rattle.

He got up. He was in a room in an old building. There were several tobacco pipes on a table, ties hanging from a nail in the wall. In one corner was a rucksack, an ice axe and high climbing boots, perfect for an expedition in the snow. The floor was covered in books piled one on top of the other. It was the room of a student, a young man who was interested in literature.

Kayat remembered that this room was on Hegenheimerstrasse. He'd come there the previous afternoon with a young woman called Fränzi Fornerod. And he'd slept for sixteen hours.

He went out into the corridor. His hostess's room was at the back. The door was open, there was no one in it. He had a look round, pure routine, he wanted to form an image of the person whose apartment he was sharing.

There was a chess set on the table. Stuck on the wall was a poster of Edvard Munch's *The Scream,* beside it a drawing, probably by the lady herself, of a marionette, an angelic girl with guileless eyes in a white nightdress, kneeling on the floor, hands and feet attached to threads that went straight up. Whoever was holding the threads couldn't be seen; the thin lines ended at the edge of the picture.

Kayat went into the kitchen and opened the fridge. It had everything: cheese, butter, milk, slices of cold meat.

He ate and drank and enjoyed two cigarettes. He liked it in this apartment, he was safe here. He had a free afternoon to look forward to, with nothing to do until the evening.

Only then, around seven, when there'd be hardly anyone out in the streets because it was so wet, would his work start. It would occupy him fully, possibly for the whole night and even beyond that.

Shortly after three the front door opened and Fräulein Fornerod came in, wearing her imitation leopard skin. She asked how he was, had he slept well.

Fine, had a great sleep, a wonderful meal and a drink, it was a very pleasant apartment.

And the trucks?

He hadn't noticed them, he was used to that.

She disappeared into her room and reappeared in a long, hand-knitted, light-blue rollneck sweater. She put a plastic bag with some heavy object inside it on the kitchen table, telling him it was from the boss, he was to take it.

Kayat took a black Browning out of the bag, briefly weighed it in his right hand, then put it back down again.

"No," he said, "I don't want to have anything to do with guns."

She looked at him out of her strangely guileless eyes in desperation, almost scared.

"Please take this gun back to your boss and tell him he'll have to find other people for that kind of work."

He slowly took her hand, which was resting beside the Browning on the table, opened it and put the palm to his lips. She smelled good. He got up, went over to her, ran his hand through her short blond hair and pulled her head back. When he tried to kiss her, she said, "Please don't. No sex, please."

He looked straight into her grey eyes and saw tears slowly running down. He leaned down over her and kissed her hair. Then he sat down again.

"I'm sorry," he said. "You're sad, but I didn't see that right away."

She bent over the table, let out two silent sobs, then wiped away the tears on the arm of her pullover.

"I know I'm stupid," she said, "but I just can't."

"No problem," he said, "love can't be forced."

"People always think I'm a sex bomb," she said, "but that's not the case at all. The sexy look's just part of my job. I'm something like a receptionist and escort for a business concern."

"And what does your boyfriend do?"

"He wants to be a writer. He's left me."

The tears appeared in her eyes again, hanging on her eyelashes. "He said he can't write when he's with me. Because I'm frigid."

The tears dropped onto the table.

"Your boyfriend's stupid," Kayat said, "no one's frigid. A pipe-smoker and a mountain-climber's nothing for a woman like you. And certainly not a writer. They only think of themselves. Find yourself someone else."

"He despises me because I'm working for that man, that firm. But I have to earn money somewhere. I pay for the apartment and the running costs so that he has time for his writing. But it just hasn't worked out. He couldn't write while he was with me."

"I beg you, please don't start crying again. It hurts me to see tears coming from eyes like yours."

"What I need is peace and quiet." She swallowed twice. "I think it's just hurt pride. He said I was a stuck-up prig."

"The most attractive prig I've ever seen."

"Please stop making these suggestive remarks. I think I'm simply not made for love. That doesn't matter, or does it?"

He shrugged, looking at her.

She put her left hand on the back of his, and brushed it three times with her fingertips. "I'm a wounded woman, do you see? I need a bit of time. Perhaps it will be all right then."

Taking back his hand, he stroked her hair. "How about a game of chess?" he asked.

"I'd like that. My boyfriend would never play with me. He said chess was the plague of capitalism by definition: occupying spaces, shutting off channels, exploiting pawns..."

"How often did you play together?"

"Just three times, then it was all over."

"And who won?"

"I did, every time." She gave a hearty laugh. "You think he couldn't stand that?"

Again he shrugged and she fetched the board and the pieces from the other room.

Kayat started with the white queen's pawn. Then he moved to c4. She declined the Queen's Gambit; instead she moved the knight to f6.

They played for more than two hours, slowly, thinking out each move until they were left with only their kings and two pawns, which were blocking each other.

"Now I can begin to understand your boyfriend not wanting to play chess," Kayat said. "You're fiendishly good at it."

She was red in the face. "I'd have won if I hadn't withdrawn the bishop from d5."

"So why did you withdraw it?"

"Because of the castle on a7."

"You see, you were afraid for your castle. Rightly so, if my memory's correct."

She nodded. "But I still should have tried it. Another game?"

He looked at the clock. It was just after six.

"I'm sorry," he said, "but I have to get on with my job."

"Perhaps tomorrow afternoon at the same time?"

"I'm sorry, that's not going to be possible. I've no idea how long my job is going to last. And I'll leave as soon as it's finished."

"The room's there if ever you want it," she said, the delightful smile playing round her lips again.

"Thank you very much. I'll take the bag and the keys to the house and apartment. You never know."

She looked at the gun on the table. Two vertical lines appeared on her forehead, just above the bridge of her nose. "Oh yes," she said, "you definitely have to take the gun, the boss said." There was a firm look in her grey eyes.

"Tell your boss that if he wants to kill someone he should do it himself."

"He won't like to hear that. He'll be telling me off again."

She was standing in the kitchen doorway, arms crossed, eyes lowered. He went over to her and kissed her on the forehead. "When I'm in Basel again, I'll come and see you and we'll have a return game. Agreed?"

She looked up, slightly startled, and nodded.

"And there's something else. I'd very much like to give you a piece of advice, but only if you want to hear it, of course."

She nodded again, giving him a smile of happy anticipation.

"You're a very bright woman, and you're well aware of that. But don't keep playing the artless country wench."

She smiled like an angel with her guileless child's eyes. "I can almost believe you're a macho man," she said. "The last real macho on this earth. That's not modern anymore, haven't you noticed that?"

He bowed politely, opened the door and went out, closing it carefully behind him. The first thing he had to do now was to find the American car, the white vintage car with the dark-red top. It would be parked somewhere in the vicinity of Lörracherstrasse.

Erika Waldis was walking along Lörracherstrasse to her apartment. The pavement was clear of snow. The slush was still knee-deep in the gutter. In a parked car there was a man sitting smoking a curved pipe and reading a book.

That didn't bother her, she had other concerns. Again and again throughout the day she'd been thinking of the visit from the policeman the previous evening, of his questions about the diamonds, of his warning. She knew that he was right. Of course Erdogan was in danger and as his girlfriend she was as well. She had the piece of paper with the telephone numbers in her handbag. But she hadn't rung him, she couldn't bring herself to do it.

She'd bought special-offer salmon and white bread, she wanted to spoil Erdogan. In the children's department she'd found a toy sheep made of black wood with its head and back covered in genuine sheep's wool. She was going to put it on the table in front of him, a present that would show him her true love.

As she climbed the stairs she lost heart for a moment.

What if he wasn't there at all? If he'd already fled to his home in Turkey with the diamonds? In that case she'd have lost him for good. He would never come back to Switzerland and she couldn't go and look for him in Turkey. And who was she? The wife to whom he was legally married, and whom he couldn't simply abandon? No, there was another woman who had that role, she herself was only tolerated, someone who could be repudiated at any time. Moreover, she was fourteen years older than him, still in good shape, she thought, healthy and pretty, but for all that about to turn into an old woman soon.

She loved him the way she'd never loved another man. Because he was friendly, clever and reliable. And because he smelt of myrrh. He was well off with her, better off than his colleagues who shared a three-room apartment with five others. So he was unlikely to leave her in the foreseeable future unless something exceptional happened. But those diamonds were exceptional and that was why she hated them.

The best thing would be for the diamonds to disappear, just like that, vanish without trace, without any fuss, just as they'd appeared, and that would be that. But there was no way of involving the police. If she'd rung the police that would have been to betray him and Erdogan's love would have turned into hate.

She went into the apartment, determined to fight.

Erdogan was sitting on the settee watching TV. Beside him was his bulging suitcase, the two locks shut and a leather safety belt round it. Erika went over to the table, tore the sheep out of the packaging and put it down in front of him. "*Koyun*," she said, "that's our sheep."

159

He looked at her, baffled, picked the sheep up, looked at it and put it down again.

"There's smoked salmon," she said, "from Norway. Special offer."

She went into the kitchen, put the kettle on, poured some powdered tea into the pot. She was trying to compose herself. That suitcase. Packed ready to go. And he hadn't had a word to say about the sheep.

She put the salmon on the sideboard, thinly cut orange-coloured slices with a delicate scent of smoke and fish. Fresh bread to go with it. And there was an opened bottle of capers in the fridge.

But he was going to leave. He'd packed without a word to her.

She realized she still had her coat and headscarf on. She'd fled into the kitchen at the sight of that suitcase. She just didn't want to see it.

She went back into the living room, turned off the TV and unbuttoned her coat.

"Where are the diamonds?" she asked.

He stared at her, he was afraid. "In my locker in Hochbergerstrasse."

"Why?"

"They've looked there already. They won't go back again."

"Why've you packed your case?" It was turning into a real interrogation, but she wasn't bothered by that.

"I'm flying to Izmir the day after tomorrow, the 11.30 from Zurich-Kloten."

She went white as snow. "What about me?"

"You can come too. I'd like you to come. I'll ask Muhammed Ali if there's still a seat going. I'm sure there'll be one left."

He was lying and he knew she'd seen that.

"I'll go and get the diamonds from the changing room on Saturday morning, then we'll drive to Kloten together, get on the plane and fly off. Agreed?"

"And you think they'll let you leave, just like that? They know you've got the diamonds, they'll assume you'll try to go to Turkey with them and they'll kill you before you can get on that plane."

"No," he said. "They don't know what I'm going to do. They don't know I'm going to leave as soon as tomorrow. I'm quicker than them. And I'll swallow the diamonds."

The kettle whistled in the kitchen. She went in, switched off the hotplate and filled the teapot, which she left there and went back into the living room.

"Right," she said. "Now you're going to phone the policeman who was here yesterday. He said we could call him any time of the day or night." She took the slip of paper out of her pocket and put it on the table.

"No. I love you, you know that. You're a good woman for me." He looked at her, an honest look, straight in the eye, and she believed him. "But I have to keep these diamonds. There's no other way, even if they want to kill me. These diamonds are more important than me and you. I've got children and I want them to be rich, not poor."

She said nothing. She knew things were the way he'd said.

"You can come with me if you want. My wife knows that I live with another woman over here. There are nice hotels in Selçuk, it's a good place to have a holiday. I'll pay for all of that. I'll also pay for the car. And I'll give you some money so that you can start up some business or other. A dry-cleaner's or something like that. Here in Basel or in

Selçuk. I'll come and see you. I don't want to lose you and you'll still be my girlfriend."

Fine words, Erika thought. Good words, if he means them seriously. Money for a dry-cleaner's, not bad. Selçuk in February, spring coming, the flowers in bloom, the air getting warm. She thought about it, began to hope.

"I mean it seriously," he said.

"What's the month when the storks come back?" she asked.

"The end of April, sometimes early May. You'll have to stay that long. You'll be in danger here, once I've gone. They'll keep an eye on you, keep pestering you. If you come with me, I'll protect you. You'll be safe in Selçuk."

She was trembling all over, she needed to sit down.

"I'm a man of my word," he said.

Then the telephone rang, once, twice, three times. At the fourth ring she got up and went over.

"No," Erdogan said, "there's no one here. Don't answer. Just leave it."

He stayed where he was, showed no sign of trying to stop her, just sat there, rigid with terror.

Erika lifted the receiver.

It was the voice she knew. "Listen, I need your Turkish friend, I've an important message for him."

Erika waved him over, but Erdogan stayed seated. Taking off her headscarf and wrapping it round the receiver, she went over to him.

"You have to talk to him," she whispered, "absolutely. You have to negotiate. Otherwise he'll just keep on at you."

Pulling him up by his sleeve, she dragged him across the room, took the headscarf off the receiver and put it in his hand.

"Yes," Erdogan said, "what is it? What do you want from me?"

"You know that very well, my friend," the voice said, and Erika could hear every word. "We got to know each other yesterday evening. You were sitting in a splendid convertible with a red top. How did you come by that?"

"It belongs to my girlfriend," Erdogan said in a strained voice, large drops of sweat on his face.

"It does, does it?" the voice said. "So you're already giving away cars. Isn't that a bit premature? Surely you haven't sold the diamonds yet?"

"I don't know anything about any diamonds. Not a thing."

"Now you just listen to me, my friend. In exactly fifteen minutes I'll be at the door of your apartment. And you'll hand over the diamonds to me. Otherwise things will be bad for you. And for your girlfriend as well. Understood?"

"Yes," Erdogan said. He heard the other man put the receiver down.

Erika pulled out the slip of paper. "Right," she said, "things are getting dangerous now and it's no fun anymore. You'll call the police, they'll be here in ten minutes."

Erdogan put on his coat, then his boots and picked up the suitcase. "Off we go now," he said. "Come on."

"You're crazy," she shouted, "you'll ruin everything, idiot that you are."

But he'd already left, he was out, going down the stairs, she could hear his boots on the steps. She hesitated, but only for a moment. She looked at the numbers on the slip of paper, then put it in her pocket. She got a nightie out of the chest of drawers, fetched her toilet things from the bathroom, stuck the sheep in the bag. She thought for a moment, got her passport and some money, locked the apartment door and went down the dark stairs.

Erdogan was in the passage to the courtyard, she could hardly see him.

"Off we go," he hissed, "hurry up. They're waiting outside in the street."

"You're crazy," she whispered, "you've gone completely round the bend."

"We'll go across the courtyard and find a way out over there. Then we'll go to the car in Hammerstrasse and clear off."

"You've seen too many crime movies. It's affected your brain."

They stomped through the slush past the carpenter's. There were drops falling from the roof and the woodstacks. The wood smelt good, it was pine.

They stopped at the wall separating the two properties. It was at least six feet high.

"You'll never get me over that," Erika whispered, "I'm much too fat. And it's sure to have bits of broken glass in the top."

"Just a mo," he said and disappeared round the back of the woodpile, reappearing almost straight away with a ladder. "I knew where that was hung. I kept my eyes open."

He propped the ladder up against the wall, she climbed up and ran her hand over the top. "A layer of ice," she said, "but no glass." She sat astride the wall and watched him climb up with the heavy suitcase, swing the ladder over to the other side and climb down. She followed him slowly, one rung after the other. "It's just like in the Wild West," she whispered once she'd reached the ground. "What are we going to do with the ladder?"

"Leave it there. Off we go now. We're halfway there."

They set off and came to a door. He pushed the handle down, the door opened. "Bit of luck," he grinned.

They went down the passage, past waist-high dustbins. Then they were out in the street. Grabbing her by the upper arms, he shook her, shouting in her ear, "We've done it!"

She felt a wave of affection for him. He was like a little rascal taking her on an adventure.

They headed off to the right, pretty quickly. Erika was panting. She could still feel the damp from the wall on her calves. He didn't look back, just straight ahead, which surprised her. If they were being followed, surely their pursuer would come from behind, not in front. She herself had no time to turn round, it was hard enough to keep up with him, but she was determined to do that, come what may.

The streets were empty. Once a vehicle drove past. It was the van of a firm of cleaners, the name was clear to see on the side. After a few minutes they saw the American car ahead on the right. It was in a no-parking area, there was a parking ticket on the windshield. Erdogan pulled it off, screwed it up and threw it away. He got into the driver's seat, turned the ignition on, the motor started. He grinned across at her.

"Shaken them off," he said, "they can get stuffed for all I care."

The car set off slowly down the street. Erika kept tight hold of the bag in her lap. She was breathing heavily, trying to calm down. It was all going well, just as it should, and it was exciting. But did it have to be? At her age! He was just a big kid, a gambler, it'd all end up in disaster for the pair of them.

"Where are you heading?"

"Anywhere, just getting away."

She turned round and looked out of the tiny rear window. "There's a car behind us," she said, "it's going the same way, it's following us."

"I saw it ages ago," he said, "it's just chance. It happens to be going in the same direction. No one's seen us."

"Turn off left," she commanded, "we'll go to Alsace, to Neuwiller."

He shook his head. "No, not across the border. There'll only be problems there."

"Turn left now." She said it clearly and confidently, she had herself under control again. "At this time of day there are no guards at the border crossing to Neuwiller. There aren't any once it gets dark. There'll be no difficulties at all."

She looked back again. The other car had followed them. By the light of a street lamp she saw that it was a small red car with an aerial.

"It's still behind us," she said, "it's a small red car."

"I know."

He threw the car into a bend. The engine wailed, accelerated. Erika looked back again. "It's still there," she told him, "it's a real chase and, my God, I'm stuck right in the middle of it."

He turned onto Dreirosenbrücke and stepped on the gas. The car stuck to them.

If a police patrol catches us, we'll be saved, Erika thought. Out loud she said, "Just ignore any red lights. If it follows us, then we'll know for sure."

"The foreign man has a small red car," he said. "I saw him driving round in it yesterday."

"With an aerial?"

Erdogan nodded. "But that could be a coincidence. There are hundreds of small red cars with aerials. And I'm not going to drive through a red light, because the police might get me."

He braked and crossed Voltaplatz, heading in the direction of Allschwil. "The border's a good idea," he said, "the border's a trap. If it's him, he'll be afraid of borders. He'll be more afraid of borders than I am."

The headlights of the other car stuck to them, never coming so close that they were able to get a clear view of the man at the wheel.

By the church in Allschwil, at the turning to Neuwiller, the car lights behind suddenly vanished. Erdogan turned up the narrow track, which still had ice on the surface. The car skidded, crashed into the snow piled at the side, ploughed on through it and got back onto the road.

"Dammit," he swore, "that's all I need just now. If we get stuck, he'll get us out of the car. Is he still there?"

"No, he's gone."

"Are you sure?"

"Let's stop at the top and see if he reappears."

Erdogan was bent right over the wheel. He looked as if he was trying to suck up the road with his eyes. At the top he let the car coast to a halt. His head dropped, he put his right hand on her thigh. "What now?" he whispered.

She turned round once more, even though she knew the road was clear behind them. Then she stroked his hair.

"Nothing," she said. "He's turned off, he's worried about the border."

His back started to quiver, then she heard him sobbing. He turned round to her and let his head drop down hard on her breast. She embraced him, stroked him.

"It'll all be fine," she said, "no one's going to do anything to you."

They drove on across the plateau, where there was deep snow that had been compacted by the traffic. The trunks of the trees glittered in the light of the headlamps, the shadows flitted to and fro. There was no one at the border crossing. There was a sign saying it was permitted to cross after 7 p.m. with valid papers if you were not carrying goods.

"It's a good thing he's not aware of that," Erdogan said in a strained voice. You could tell he'd been afraid. Suddenly he drummed his fingers on the steering wheel and prodded her in the side. He was laughing, giggling like mad, and he opened the window and shouted out into the night, "Get stuffed, get stuffed the lot of you!"

The car was travelling slowly and with soothing steadiness across the dark countryside. The fields were a gleaming white. Occasional trees appeared in the beam of the headlights, stunted old fruit trees with mistletoe growing on them.

They came to the village. It was quiet and sleepy. There were a few cars with Basel licence plates parked outside the inn. The stream beside it had overflowed its banks. There was shingle there, twigs, mud. Erdogan braked and let the tyres roll slowly over it. They could hear a quiet whizzing sound, as if someone was tearing silk. He parked under the trees. She looked at the illuminated front of the building, the bright areas of plaster between the dark oak timbers. It was like a house from a fairy tale that had popped up out of the *Arabian Nights*.

They had a double room free that looked out onto the stream. Boxed-in beams supported the ceiling. The floorboards creaked. Just like it had been in Weggis, Erika thought. She unpacked her nightie and put it on the blue-checked cover. She stood the sheep on the bedside table.

Erdogan was standing by the window, looking out at the road. The room was filled with the calm murmur of the stream.

"We're safe here," he said, turning back into the room. "A holiday in the country, a holiday in France. We'll do that a lot now, every weekend."

She stood opposite him. An expectant look on her face.

"I mean when I'm back from Turkey. Once I've sold the diamonds." He saw the sheep. "That's a nice present. A lovely present. Thank you."

"I'll need fifteen minutes to get ready," she said, "then we can go down and eat. It's on me."

She went into the bathroom to do herself up. It was the first time they'd stayed overnight in a hotel together and she was nervous. The room was luxurious, a first-class place for an overnight stay for businessmen and their secretaries. Next to the lavatory bowl there was even a bidet for ladies and yet she wasn't a lady. Or was she?

She examined herself in the mirror, her full, firm lips, her strong nose, which was a bit too big. Her bright eyes, half-yellow, half-green, they were what she liked best. Then her long, dark-blond hair. She should have had it cut nicely ages ago. But she'd had no idea they'd be going to France that evening, otherwise she'd definitely have made the necessary preparations. I'm not a lady, she thought, and I certainly don't want to be one. I'm a woman from the countryside who works at the checkout. And I'm quite happy with that. He has to take me the way I am, after all he's the one who invited me here, and that's that.

Despite that she did what she could to make herself look her best. She even dabbed a few drops of Fleur de Nuit, the French perfume Nelly had given her for Christmas, on her neck, and she thought she didn't look all that bad as she went back into the room.

Erdogan was lying on the bed, staring at the ceiling.

"Being rich is good," he said, "being rich makes you strong as a horse." He laughed contentedly. "No, that's wrong. Being rich makes you as strong as two horses, or even as a whole herd."

He turned his head. "Wow," he said, "you've done yourself up, you look really beautiful."

She beamed at him, stroking his forehead with its receding hairline. "I've made myself as beautiful as one can at my age. Let's go and eat, I'm hungry."

They went down the stairs as if to a celebration, she in front, he behind.

In the restaurant they were given a table looking out over the stream. They could see the convertible in the darkness, partly hidden by a tree.

"This is the second time we've gone out for a drive," Erika said, "first of all over the Gempenfluh, now to France. That was a good buy."

"True," Erdogan said, "but too conspicuous. I'll take it back tomorrow."

He saw how sad she looked at that, lowering her eyes.

"Don't feel sad," he said, taking her hand, "please don't. You're coming with me."

"What does your wife look like? Like me?"

"She's a bit shorter and a bit fatter, but yes, she's like you."

"And your three children, what are they called?"

"Memed, Elvira, Yaşar."

"Are they at school?"

"Yes, I think so. Except for Yaşar. He's too young."

He was happy to tell her things, friendly, he didn't mind talking about his family. Perhaps that would be the solution, she thought; after all, having more than one wife was permitted for Muslims.

The waiter carried a dish of roast pheasant past them.

"Look how beautiful they are," Erdogan said. "With birds it's the opposite to humans. With pheasants the cock is beautiful and colourful, not the hen."

"You think I'm beautiful and colourful?"

"Yes, very beautiful and colourful, like a cock pheasant. There you are, you're laughing again. Let's laugh today, tears will come soon enough. And we'll eat a cock pheasant together."

"No, I don't like game. And I feel sorry for a pheasant like that. Let's eat a fish together."

"That's good too, a fish."

She studied the menu. "Here, *loup de mer*. If we're not going to eat the special-offer salmon, then we'll just have to eat a *loup de mer*."

"And you won't feel sorry for it?"

"No, that's a wolf, a sea-wolf. And we'll have a bottle of Alsatian white wine to go with it."

"Beer, yes," he said, "but not wine."

"No, this time you're going to make an exception. It could be the last time," she said boldly, "that we'll be eating together."

"Who knows what tomorrow will bring? Let's drink wine."

Erika gave the order. The waiter brought an ice bucket containing the long, slim, elegant bottle. Erdogan had to take the first sip.

"I don't know anything about it," he protested, "I'll have no idea whether it's good or bad."

"You're not going to get out of it," she told him, "the monsieur tastes and tells the madame whether it's good or bad."

He took a sip, nodded, the waiter filled their glasses. Then a large serving dish was brought with a lovely big fish on it such as she'd never seen at Weggis on the Vierwaldstättersee. The only fish she was familiar with from home was perch, a greedy predator with spiny rear fins. This fish was a superior kind.

"Do you know this kind of fish? They come from the sea and you come from the seaside."

"We're farmers," he said, "we never eat fish."

"What do you eat then?"

"The things we have. Potatoes, bread, vegetables."

"And meat?"

"Meat's expensive. Perhaps a sheep now and then, on a special day, that kind of thing."

"*Koyun.*"

He nodded. "You'll have to learn about all that. I mean it seriously. You have to come with me, I'll pay for the journey and I'll show you everything."

"The children too?"

"Of course, I'll show you the children as well." He raised his glass.

"Cheers. To a long and healthy life. Is that what you say?"

"Yes. We'll drink to a lovely long and healthy life." She raised her glass.

The waiter filleted the fish and served it. They ate it with reverence and agreed that it was the best fish they'd ever tasted. The bottle they emptied, even though it took some doing – they weren't used to wine. But they felt it would be bad manners to leave such an expensive bottle half-full.

Slightly tipsy, they went up the stairs to their room. Cool, damp night air was coming in through the open window.

"You know what?" she said. "Let's just go on tomorrow, all the way to Paris, and then even further, to the sea. I'd like to hear the roar of the waves with you."

He got in beside her, carefully and lovingly. He kissed her, she kissed him back, with a shy, quick tongue. It was the way it always was, but not quite. There was something new about him. Or was it her?

"D'you know something?" she said.

"No, but tell me."

"It's better in a hotel, in a different bed."

*

Erika woke in the middle of the night. She'd been dreaming. She'd seen a fish swimming around in clear, clean water in the sea somewhere. It had been wonderful to watch it, floating, calm and proud, among the aquatic plants. Lurking on the seabed or in a cave was a giant octopus – a terrible monster, evil and vicious. The fish meant life or death to it. The monster was confident and strangely sad. And the fish was gently moving its fins.

She could hear the murmur of the stream, she could hear Erdogan breathing. Picking up her watch from the bedside table, she saw that it was shortly before three. There was a noise outside, as if someone was tearing cloth apart. She didn't move. Someone out there was making a proper job of it. Then she heard a soft whistling and hissing, like air coming out. The hissing was repeated, once, twice, three times. She got up quietly, not wanting to wake Erdogan. She didn't put the light on, she went across to the window in the dark.

The convertible was down there, half-hidden by a tree. In the glimmer of the street light she could see that the red soft top was ruined, ripped to pieces. There was no air left in the tyres, they were slashed, completely flat.

Beside it was a small red car with an aerial, its lights off. After a while the engine was switched on, quietly, no foot down on the accelerator, the driver didn't want to wake anyone. Or did he? Then the little car drove off, still without lights, a quiet shadow on the road.

Erika waited until she couldn't hear the sound of the engine anymore. She was freezing in the night air, suddenly shivering with the cold. She got back into bed beside her man, carefully, so as not to wake him, she could feel his warmth and fell asleep.

*

When Erika woke next morning, Erdogan was standing at the window looking out. She could hear the clock on the church chiming nine. She sat up.

"The car's ruined," he said dully, "someone's slashed the roof and the tyres."

"I know. I saw him."

"What? Are you crazy? Why didn't you tell me?"

"It was just before three. I woke up and looked out. It was the small red car with the aerial."

He closed the window, sat down on the bed and rested his chin on his hands. She looked at his feet. They were chubby feet. The underside of the nail of his right big toe was blue.

"It was that foreigner," he said, "he's not giving up. He's pursuing me. He always knows where I am."

"That's what I told you. The next time he calls you'll have to talk to him."

"He won't call me again, because I'm going to hide. He won't find me."

"You're just a big kid," she said, stroking his back, "but you're sweet."

He looked at her, desperate for help, in the grip of fear again.

"What's a big kid?" he asked.

"It's someone who can take tremendous pleasure in something that doesn't belong to him."

He thought it over, he was close to tears. "Neither of us will go to work today," was his conclusion. "We'll get a taxi and go and see Muhammed in the cafe. We'll stay there until

175

tomorrow morning, then we'll go to the station, get a train to Kloten and fly to Izmir. That's a good plan. D'you agree?"

She threw her arms round him and kissed him on the back of his neck. "You're stupid. I've already told you there's no chance he'll let us go unless you've handed over the diamonds. But you're very sweet, to me at least. Do you know that?"

He tried to smile despite his fear.

"Wealth doesn't make you as strong as a whole herd," he said, "wealth makes you tender and randy. That's the way things are all over the world, for men and women. And I'm not going to give up that wealth. I'm going to flee with it. And you'll flee with me. You'll help me. Agreed?"

She rocked her head slowly from side to side, considering, as if she were thinking about where they might go.

"Let's have breakfast first," she said, "I'm already late as it is. I'll phone and tell them I'm sick again, a relapse. Then we'll go to the cafe, if you like, and see what's what."

"Good. And this time tomorrow we'll be on the train to Kloten."

She took hold of her hair, gathered it at the back of her neck and pulled it over her left shoulder. "As long as he hasn't got the diamonds," she said, "you'll stay alive. That means on no account must he get his hands on the diamonds."

When they went into the restaurant they were met by a smell of fresh coffee. There was a white loaf on the table, cut into slices, crusty and light.

Madame appeared, throwing up her hands and lamenting. "Have you seen what's happened to your car? They're vandals, real hooligans, these people who hate foreigners.

They want to drive people from Basel away, terrorize them so they won't drive over into Alsace anymore. And the Baselers are our best customers. Without them I'll be closing the hotel down. But those guys don't understand that, how we're all dependent on each other. We're neighbours, you see, and we profit from each other. We belong together, we speak the same language. But just you go out and look at your car. It's horrifying."

"We've seen it already," Erika said. "It's not that bad. If you can lend us a screwdriver we'll unscrew the licence plates and take a taxi back. We'll leave the car here, if that's all right, just for a few days."

"But of course that's all right. You can even have it towed away. There's a firm of house-breakers where you come into the village. They could see to that if you like."

"We'll let you know," Erika said, a real lady now, "but first of all we'll have to consult our garage."

"As you wish. And no journalists, please. It would be a catastrophe for my business if that got into the newspapers."

"The very idea, madame!" Erika said with a friendly smile. "This kind of thing happens. There are people who hate foreigners everywhere."

The car really was in a bad way. The steering wheel was broken, the electric cables pulled out, the leather seats slit open. It was a car fit only for the scrapyard, no longer a classy limousine.

Shortly after eleven they got into the taxi Madame had ordered. They both sat in the back, close together. Erdogan was holding Erika's hand, as if he was trying to help her. But she knew he was the one who had to be protected.

The border crossing was unmanned, the taxi drove across with no problem. They turned their heads to look back several times. No one was following them.

A buzzard was perched on a walnut tree, unbelievably close, unbelievably powerful. The Black Forest, beyond the plain where Basel lay, was a dark gleam in the sunlight. Just a few patches of white could be seen on the treetops.

They drove across the town without a word. Erika's hand was on Erdogan's thigh, his face was damp with sweat.

"You don't need to be afraid," she said, "you're safe with me."

The taxi stopped outside Café Ankara. Erika paid and they got out. A few cars went by, a mother was pushing her perambulator over the pedestrian crossing. There was a screech of brakes from a truck.

The handcart of a woman selling vegetables was laden with potatoes, cabbages and carrots. The woman, fat and wearing a heavy woollen coat, was counting onions. She looked up, interested, friendly. "Do you need anything, madame?" she asked.

Erika shook her head. She took Erdogan by the hand and went up the steps into the cafe.

After a while a small red car drove past. It had an aerial sticking up on the right-hand side and stopped right beside the vegetable cart. The man at the wheel looked across into the cafe. He saw the notice that said that at 11.30 a.m. on Saturday there was a flight from Zurich-Kloten to Izmir. The Turkish seasonal worker Erdogan Civil was standing at the counter being given a plane ticket.

The man at the wheel put the car into first gear and drove off. He parked the car just a bit further on, picked up the phone and tapped in 123 63 20. A powerful, sonorous male voice replied. "Hello?" it said in affable tones.

"Kayat here, Guy Kayat."

A pause. Heavy breathing. Then the voice again, firm and no longer affable. "I don't know anyone of that name."

"I absolutely had to get in touch," Kayat whispered. "I'm sorry. I'll make it brief. A Turk called Erdogan Civil has the diamonds, he fished them out of the sewers. He intends to take a flight tomorrow, 11.30 from Kloten to Izmir. He'll have the diamonds on him."

Another pause. Again the deep breaths. "The swine," the voice said quietly, "that's not allowed."

Peter Hunkeler was lying on the camp bed in his office, wrapped in a blanket. He looked at the maple out in the yard. The crows had gone, flown off, vanished at the crack of dawn while he was still dreaming.

It had been a restless night's sleep. He'd turned over and over, and kept rolling himself up in the foetal position, his head full of the craziest ideas. They didn't get him anywhere, he didn't have the solution, and without the solution he couldn't do anything, couldn't help.

He had wondered several times about taking Civil into custody in order to protect him. But what pretext should he use for that? That the little man was suspected of having found some diamonds without reporting it as regulations demanded? But how was he going to prove that? And what about Kayat, what about the intended recipient of the

179

goods? He would be warned and withdraw behind even stronger defences.

Hunkeler still hadn't given up hope of finding that man. It was easy enough to catch the little couriers, who risked several years in prison for peanuts. But that didn't get them anywhere. Behind those wretched figures there were hundreds of others equally prepared to risk losing their freedom for a few thousand francs.

But the people behind them, who knew all about finance and could earn hundreds of thousands with a few strokes of the pen, without ever getting their fingers dirty, they were as good as untouchable. You almost never caught them, and if you did chance to get your hands on one, you could never prove anything against them.

He just had to let things take their course. That was paralysing, a strain on the nerves, it demanded total concentration. He was waiting for a call from Erika Waldis. She would call at the moment when things got too dangerous for her, of that he was sure.

He was covered in sweat, he felt feverish. He ought to have shaved and had a shower, but he didn't want to.

He got out of bed, picked up the phone and ordered breakfast with tea from Café Kastell. Then he lay back down on the camp bed, rolled himself up in the blanket, his head in his arms, and tried to force himself to think logically.

Five minutes later the telephone rang. It was Haller reporting that neither Erdogan Civil nor Frau Waldis had left the apartment that morning. He'd phoned and let it ring more than twenty times but no one had answered. He had gone up and thumped on the door, no one had opened it. He'd searched the joiner's at the back for clues and had found some. There was a ladder leaning against the wall that separated the two properties, and it was on the other side, the way they'd escaped. "Out through the backyard," he groaned, "while I'm watching at the front, arsehole that I am. Should I break into the apartment?"

"No," Hunkeler said, putting the phone down.

There was a knock at the door. A woman from the cafe came in with the breakfast tray. She was followed by the state prosecutor. Suter was agitated, stunned.

"Well then, Inspector," he barked, "how are things going? Well, I hope? But don't let me interrupt. Eat your breakfast in peace, enjoy your meal."

He sat down at the table. Clearly he had something up his sleeve, something decisive, conclusive.

Hunkeler carefully poured himself a cup of tea. He took a sip and spread butter on a slice of bread.

"Things aren't going well," he said. "We're assuming that a Turkish seasonal worker found the diamonds in the sewers. I've just heard from Haller that the man has disappeared along with his girlfriend. The birds have flown, just like those crows."

"Like what, if I may ask?"

"Like those crows," Hunkeler said, "big black birds. And Kayat hasn't resurfaced. The whole lot of them have disappeared and I'm left with nothing to work on. All I can do is wait and that's what I am doing."

"Crows, black birds, what's the point of all that?" Suter was gasping. "You're sitting round doing nothing, while these mafia guys are giving us the runaround. And the obvious course, the one sensible thing, is what you're not doing. I've got something to tell you. Shortly before eight this morning, while you were presumably stretched out on your camp bed, weary from your unsettled, difficult life, a local jeweller called Bernett called. And do you know what he told me?"

Hunkeler stopped chewing and shook his head.

"He told me that three days ago, on that snowy Tuesday morning, while you were sleeping off the drink, a strange couple came into his store: a rather fat, fifty-year-old Swiss woman and a small, considerably younger foreigner who looked Turkish. And do you know what the two of them wanted, if I may ask?"

Again Hunkeler shook his head.

"They wanted to sell two diamonds to Herr Bernett. Two very good examples such as you seldom see, each one worth tens of thousands of Swiss francs. So what do you say to that, eh?"

Hunkeler put his hand in his jacket pocket, took out his packet of cigarettes, lit one, took a drag, coughed.

"You're speechless now, eh? You're coughing like a cow that's eaten too much fresh clover, if I may put it like that."

Hunkeler grinned. The analogy didn't make sense and Suter was aware of that as well.

"*Tant pis*," he barked, "what's the point of these analogies? Cough as much as you like. Go ahead and ruin your health if you must. But don't forget your duty. You're squatting here, as indolent as a philosopher, regretting times past. You're a washed-up idealist who thought he could put the world to rights. And all the while the stones you should have seized four days ago in Badischer Station are being offered for sale in broad daylight on the streets of Basel. Have you any explanation for that, if I may ask?"

Hunkeler stubbed out his cigarette. "I have no explanation," he said, "but I need a search warrant."

Suter's heavy hand hit the table. "At last. And high time too. Search that Turk's apartment, turn everything upside down, get hold of those diamonds. And arrest those gangsters at last."

He stood up, glared at the camp bed and was about to go out when Hunkeler said:

"One more thing: I suggest we keep the Infex phone lines under surveillance."

"What's that? You still suspect Dr Zeugin? Have you gone out of your mind? That's your revolutionary past coming through again. Always against the rich and powerful, eh? Your version of that communist Dutschke's method of infiltrating the institutions in order to establish the revolution," he bellowed, his face bright red. "You're in the wrong place here, in the wrong institution. It's out of the question. No bugging of Infex. None, and that's final."

He went out, slamming the door behind him.

Hunkeler had been treated like dirt and he felt he deserved it. Things kept happening he had no idea about and he was always one step behind. Or was that not the case? Perhaps he was already there before the others arrived?

He picked up the telephone and dialled Schneeberger's number.

"We've got a search warrant for Civil's apartment," he said. "Search it but don't break anything. There's an aquarium with black sand on the bottom. Have a look there. And one more thing: one of you is to take up position outside Infex in Gempenfluhstrasse and see what's going on, whether Zeugin goes in or out, whether Kayat arrives or the leopard woman turns up. But very discreetly, please, don't intervene, Zeugin's a big cheese."

"I'll do that," Schneeberger said, "I know the lady. And what are you actually going to be doing all this time. Are you OK, if I may ask?" He laughed but it was more of a nasty snigger.

"No," Hunkeler said, "I'm not OK. Clearly everything I do is wrong."

"That's true," Schneeberger said, "but don't worry too much about it. We all know you're a real heavy guy."

"Thanks," Hunkeler said.

Erika Waldis spent the rest of the day in Café Ankara. She sat on the bench in the corner with a glass of the strong tea she liked very much. She watched Erdogan at the counter negotiating with the landlord, who appeared to be called Muhammed Ali.

"Everything's OK," he said as he sat down beside her, "the plane to Izmir's only half-full." He gave her a wink with his left eye, raised his arm and put his hand on her shoulder.

They had vegetable soup seasoned with unusual spices and soft white bread. "Do you like it?" he asked.

"Yes," she said, "it's very good, the tea as well."

He gave her a friendly, almost patronizing nod, but she could tell he didn't feel right. Was it the fear that was still getting to him or something else?

"You're safe here," he said, pointing to the men playing cards. "They'll all help me. No one's going to take anything away from me here, and you're protected, just like in a big family."

They sat there in silence – a couple who belonged together. None of the men looked over at them. They'd given her a friendly nod when she came in and Erdogan had introduced her. Some had given her a greeting she couldn't understand. She was clearly not unwelcome; after all, she was Erdogan's girlfriend. But it had immediately struck her that she was the only woman in the room. And she was more and more coming to feel that she wasn't there at all.

She looked out at the vegetable cart on the pavement. The old woman was unscrewing a thermos flask and she was having trouble with it. The lid was tight. She tried again, bending forward with the effort and finally she managed it. She carefully poured some for herself, drank, unpacked a sausage sandwich and took a bite. She chewed slowly, it was clear she had dentures. It took her a long time to finish the sandwich. Then she folded up the paper and stuck it in a plastic bag hanging from the axle. She poured herself another cup, you could see how she enjoyed the warmth of the coffee, screwed the top back on the thermos and put it on the cart. Finally she crossed her arms, putting her hands up the bottom of her sleeves, and waited.

"I'm going out for a moment," Erika said, "I need some vegetables."

Erdogan gave her a blank look. "Just be careful," he said, "it's dangerous out in the street. It's better if you stay in here."

She gave him a smile and went out. She bought a pound of onions, two pounds of carrots and a large white cabbage.

The woman weighed out everything carefully, putting weights on the scales until the two hands were level, packed up the onions, carrots and cabbage in newspaper and put them all in a plastic bag.

"What's the weather going to do?" she asked in her broad Alsace German. "This bastard weather, it's all mixed up. First it's as cold as January, then it's as warm as May. The whole field's under water, but what can you do, madame? That makes *huit francs*, please."

Erika paid and looked round to see if there was anything suspicious. Everything was normal, cars, bicycles, people on foot. Everything was lovely. And the vegetables from Alsace were stacked up in the cart, ready to be sold, prepared, cooked and eaten.

When she got back to the cafe, Erdogan was sitting at another table with two men playing cards. He got up and took her to the bench, fetched his coat that he'd hung on a chair and handed it to her.

"Have a lie-down," he said, "and wrap yourself up in my coat. The best thing would be for you to sleep for a bit. We're off tomorrow morning."

He gave her a wink with his left eye again and went back to his cards.

She lay down and wrapped herself up. She could hear the men talking, she could hear the music that played continuously. She liked that music, she knew that it was ballads, songs about love and death, popular songs about men and women who were in love, who left each other, who betrayed each other. She would have loved to be able to understand those foreign words, both gay and sad, that were sung again and again with such fervour.

When she woke up, it was dark outside. The music was still playing. The babble of voices had increased, the cafe was packed right down to the last seat with men smoking, playing cards, talking. Only the corner where she'd been sleeping was empty.

She picked up Erdogan's jacket, slowly, so that no one noticed. She searched for and found the keys to his locker and took them out. Then she got up. She took the coat, the suitcase and the plastic bag with the vegetables and went over to Erdogan.

"Thanks for your jacket," she said. "I'm not going to spend the night here, it's too loud."

He looked up, embarrassed. The men were suddenly silent, all of them.

"You can't spend the night in our apartment," he said, "it's impossible, it's too dangerous."

"I'll go to Nelly's. There I'll be as safe as here. I'll be back tomorrow at seven."

It was clear that he felt uncomfortable. He thought for a moment. "Right then, if you want. Until seven. But take a taxi, not the tram."

She would have liked to give him a kiss, on the top of his head, on the lips, but she didn't dare.

"*Güle güle*," she said attempting a smile as she used the Turkish for "goodbye". He didn't get up, he stayed seated, and she went out.

There were still quite a few people out in the street. A warm wind pressed the bottom of her coat against her calves. She went down to the square with its taxi rank and climbed into a cab. "Hochbergerstrasse," she said, "the sewage workers' changing room, please."

The driver thought. "That must be the city waterworks," he muttered grumpily, "the Board of Works, or whatever it's called."

"Just go to Hochbergerstrasse, I'll recognize where it is then."

The car set off, drove through the dark streets and turned into Hochbergerstrasse. She looked back just once, she didn't care if she was being followed.

"There it is. Please wait, I'll be back in five minutes."

The driver reached back, opened the door and she got out. "The clock's still running," he said. "Leave your bags in the car, please."

She crossed the forecourt and opened the door. She didn't switch on the light, the beam from the lamp outside was enough. She opened Erdogan's locker, took out the bag with the diamonds, stuffed it in her coat pocket and locked the door.

The driver was watching her, eyes screwed up, when she got back in. "What have you been doing in there, if I may ask? Looking for mushrooms at this time of the year?"

"That's none of your business," she said calmly and gave him Nelly's address.

She was almost crying as he drove on; with her hand in her coat pocket she could feel the edges of the diamonds. Strong as a horse, she thought, strong as a whole herd of wild mustangs, their manes fluttering, the earth trembling.

But she stayed firm.

Nelly was already in her pyjamas when she arrived. "You?" she asked. "Have you had an argument?"

"I'm tired," Erika said. "I'll tell you everything later. Can I sleep here?"

"Always, you know that."

"I need to go to the toilet," Erika said.

"Make yourself at home. By the way, there's a thriller on after the news. We can watch that if you like."

Erika went to the toilet and locked the door. She took the plastic bag with the diamonds out of her coat pocket and emptied it down the toilet. They lay there in the shallow water, glittering, with their shimmer of blue. Like little silver pebbles, she thought. She lifted the lever, there was the roar of the water flushing and the stones had gone. She chucked the plastic bag in the trash can, washed her hands and had a look at herself in the mirror. Her nose was still too big but there was a yellowish-green gleam in her eyes that she liked.

That evening Hunkeler was close to despair. There had been no movement, no clue had been found, no Frau Waldis had rung. The search of the apartment had not brought anything, no diamonds, no suspicious address, nothing.

He felt queasy and decrepit with age. An old goat, brain soft, cock soft, knees soft. And yet he was sure what he'd done was absolutely right.

He'd drunk three pots of tea and eaten a block of chocolate. He hadn't washed, hadn't shaved. Let things grow as they liked – hair, fingernails and toenails. He had nothing but contempt for all this growing, for his increasing body odour. He did actually stink like an old goat and he couldn't care less.

Around 9 p.m. a policeman from St Louis, just over the border in Alsace, phoned. He apologized at length for calling so late, he'd had too many problems with foreigners, above all Algerians and Moroccans, they were like flies, sometimes here, sometimes there, almost impossible to pin down. Moreover, the police in the surrounding villages were seriously underfunded, you could hardly ever find one and the villagers had got into the habit of dealing with things themselves. "They never report anything, they're thick as thieves and look on the police as the enemy. And if we happen to have a speed check because people are driving at over a hundred on the main road, they warn each other by flashing their headlights. How can you catch anyone then?"

"Difficult, difficult," Hunkeler said. "But what is it you want to tell me?"

"Right then." The policeman from St Louis cleared his throat to embark on a serious speech. "Last night, outside the auberge in Neuwiller, an old American car, white with a red top, was totally destroyed. The landlady guesses the motive was hatred of foreigners, but it could have been something else, which is why I'm calling. The car had a Basel registration."

"Could you give me the number, please?"

"I'm afraid not. The licence plates were unscrewed and taken away by the owners. A Frau Waldis, she registered under that name at reception. And she was accompanied by a man from the Balkans or Turkey."

"Thank you very much," Hunkeler said, "we'll call back if we find out anything that could be of interest to you."

He put the phone down. At last, he thought.

Neuwiller, Alsace, why was Civil travelling to France? And who destroyed his car? Is he going to fly from Bâle-Mulhouse? Does Kayat know that, is he pursuing him?

He ordered a pot of coffee and called the Swissair office at Bâle-Mulhouse airport. No, there was nothing they could tell him. No plane was setting off for a Turkish destination the next day, nor the day after. But just a minute – from Zurich-Kloten there was a charter flight to Izmir the next day, at 11.30 a.m.

"Can you retrieve the passenger list?" Hunkeler asked, the fingers of his left hand drumming on the beechwood.

"Sorry, no. But they might perhaps be able to do that in Zurich-Kloten."

There was a knock on the door, the woman was bringing the coffee. Hunkeler thanked her and gave her a friendly smile, wondering whether he should tell her she was an angel.

He didn't. He picked up the receiver and called Zurich-Kloten.

It was difficult, a friendly woman's voice told him, to get the passenger list for a charter flight at this late hour. But it wasn't impossible. He should phone the Zurich police or talk to the airport police.

Hunkeler called the airport police. He told them that it was highly likely that on the next day – Saturday – a Turkish national called Erdogan Civil was going to be on a charter flight to Izmir. He was to be observed during check-in and arrested shortly before take-off. And one more thing: they urgently needed to know where this Herr Civil had bought his flight ticket.

Then Hunkeler tipped his chair back, put his feet up on the edge of the desk, smoked, drank coffee and waited.

At 10.50 p.m. Schneeberger called in, enthusiastic and in a good mood.

"I've seen her," he said, "there can be no doubt, it was her."

"Who?" Hunkeler asked – a stupid question.

"The woman with the leopard-skin coat," Schneeberger said, "who else? There's only one woman like that in the whole of Basel."

"And where is she now?"

"Off on her bicycle. I tell you…"

"Are you crazy, you idiot?" Hunkeler shouted. "You are and ever will be the station arsehole."

Now Schneeberger felt insulted. "But you said be discreet, don't take any action, it's a big fish we're dealing with."

"Dr Zeugin's a big fish, but not that woman."

He slammed the receiver back down, so furious he could have eaten it.

He sat upright, hands flat on his knees. I am calm and relaxed, he murmured, and my head is heavy and warm… and my stomach and my balls.

It was no use. He knocked his chair over, slapped his hand on the table, hard enough to hurt, lay down on the camp bed and curled up like a little child.

After a while he'd calmed down and started thinking things over. "Well now," he said, out loud, "our Dr Zeugin does have a whole lot of interesting employees."

The next morning on the dot of seven – it was a normal Saturday morning, not much traffic out in the streets, the level of the Rhine was still higher than usual, the air had a smell of spring – Erika Waldis was walking up Colmarerstrasse to Café Ankara. She was carrying her bag and the plastic bag with the vegetables. She felt good, she'd slept well, back to back with Nelly in the double bed. They'd had breakfast together, without saying very much, they'd realized that they still liked each other, that they could depend on each other.

She went into the cafe quietly, she didn't want to draw attention to herself. She could see Erdogan, sitting at a table with a cup of tea. Standing beside him was Muhammed Ali, who was going on at him. When he heard the door open, he stopped abruptly, as if he'd been caught out. Erika went over to Erdogan and tried to give him a kiss. He pushed her aside.

"Good that you've come," he said, "we were getting worried."

"Who's this 'we'?" she asked.

He looked up at Muhammed Ali, unsure of himself, he was very pale. "That foreigner's still after us," he said, "after you, after me. I'm going to take a taxi to the changing room on Hochbergerstrasse. Then there are a few other things I have to sort out. I'll be back here in an hour's time to fetch you. Then we'll go to the station, together, and take the train to Kloten. Everything OK?"

"No," she said, finding it difficult not to tell the truth, "I'm not staying here in this cafe. I don't like it here. I'll go to the apartment. I'll be at the station in an hour's time, perhaps, who knows? Did you sleep well?"

"You're talking in a strange way." He looked at her, forlorn, naked fear in his eyes. "It's too dangerous to go back to the apartment. You're staying here."

"No. I'm going where I live, where I feel at home. And you're at home there as well."

193

He stood up. "Right then. At the station in an hour's time."

He said farewell to Muhammed Ali, picked up his suitcase and went out with her, scanning the area around them. "Everything's OK," he whispered with a wink.

"I'll go with you until you're in the taxi," she said, "my tram stop's down by the taxi rank."

Erdogan hesitated. It was clear he didn't want to put her in unnecessary danger, big kid that he was, stubborn as a mule. Or did he simply want to get rid of her?

"Come on, off we go then," he said.

They hurried down Colmarerstrasse. He was almost running, she was panting.

"You go on ahead," she said, "I can't go that fast. I don't imagine anyone's going to steal you."

Giving a brief nod he went on without stopping and crossed the road a few yards further on, running straight out in front of a small red car with an aerial that had come driving along at tremendous speed and braked with a squeal of tyres. The bumper caught him on the right leg, he fell over, got up quickly and tried to run off. It was too late. A muscular bald guy had got out of the car and grabbed him by the arm. A second man in a pale camel-hair coat came over with quick, almost elegant steps and punched him in the stomach. Erdogan doubled up. They dragged him into the car, closed the doors and drove off.

"Murderers, thieves, criminals!" Erika shouted. She had run as quickly as possible to help her man, to support him. She was too late.

A pensioner on a bicycle had stopped, his chin quivering with excitement, spittle dripping from his lips. He helped her gather up the carrots that had fallen out of the plastic bag.

"That was an abduction," he said, "just like in Chicago. I saw everything. We have to phone the police."

Erika picked up the sack, the bag and the suitcase, which were lying in the gutter. One of the two locks had burst open, but the leather strap had kept everything in.

She went across to Café Ankara as fast as she could. The vegetable woman was setting up her cart. "What's the panic?" she asked as she saw Erika rushing past.

She opened the door, put the suitcase down and went straight to the telephone. There she dialled the first number Inspector Peter Hunkeler had given her. When he replied she spoke loud and clear, so that he'd hear everything perfectly. "They've grabbed him, two men. They beat him up. He thinks the diamonds are in his locker in Hochbergerstrasse, but they're not there."

"Where are they then?"

"I'll tell you that later. They'll torture him and he'll take them to the changing room. You have to get there and save him, at once."

"Thanks," Hunkeler said, putting the phone down.

She suddenly felt dead tired, she had to sit down, her knees had started to quiver. She was trembling as she'd never trembled before. She put her arms round her head and swayed to and fro.

Someone came over and stood beside her. It was Muhammed Ali. He put a glass of tea down in front of her, looking shy and uncertain.

"What's happened? Did they grab him?"

She nodded, pulled out her handkerchief and wiped away the tears. "It's his own fault. He's the most stubborn mule I've ever seen, the idiot."

"You phoned the police, didn't you?"

She nodded again and sipped the tea.

"And now? What will they do to him?"

"They won't kill him, because he doesn't know where the diamonds are. They'll only kill him once they've got the diamonds. And they'll never get them."

"Erdogan's my friend," he said quietly, "and you're his wife here in Switzerland. You're under my protection as long as he's not here. You can rely on me, I keep my word. But tell me where the diamonds are."

She put down her empty glass, took out her powder compact and dabbed her cheeks. She went over her lips with her lipstick and carefully checked how she looked in her pocket mirror. Everything OK, no tears anymore, eyes as bright as amber.

"I'll tell you that later. Now's not the right time. I'm going home to wait for my man."

She stood up, picked up the suitcase and the bags, and went out.

A small red car drove quickly along Hochbergerstrasse and stopped in the forecourt of the sewage workers' changing room. The driver, a youngish Middle Eastern-looking man in a light-coloured camel-hair coat, got out and tipped the seat forward. A muscular bald guy got out of the back seat, stretched his torso, spat on the ground, leaned back down into the car and dragged a little man out; his left eye was swollen. A thin line of blood ran down his chin.

"Right then," the bald guy said, "now show us the diamonds."

The three of them went to the door. The little man was looking for something in his jacket pocket. He shook his head. "I've lost the keys. I've no idea where they are, honestly."

The bald guy took a couple of steps back, ran up and hit the door with the full power of his right shoulder. The door swung open, the three of them went in.

A dark-blue British-made limousine drove slowly onto the forecourt. At the wheel was a plump man. He switched the engine off and waited, looking across at the open door of the changing room. A grating noise could be heard from inside, a quiet grating, as if someone were breaking open a lock. Then there was silence.

The man in the limousine was nervously drumming his fingers on the steering wheel. He opened the door so that he could hear better. He saw the three men come out again, the bald guy first, dragging the little man behind him. He shook him, slapped him across the face.

"You swine, you thief," he shouted, "I'll thrash you till the diamonds come out."

The little man raised his hand to swear an oath: "On my mother's life I swear that I don't know where the diamonds are."

At that the man in the limousine got out and went over to the three of them. "What's going on?" he asked. "Have you got them at last?"

"No," the bald guy said. "The swine told us a load of lies."

"What do you mean by that?" the man asked, pale with fury.

"I mean," the bald guy said, "that there aren't any diamonds in his locker."

The fat man gasped. "That's criminal," he screamed, "that's not allowed. You're living here in the free country of Switzerland and stealing isn't allowed here." Putting his hand in his jacket pocket, he took out a black Browning and hit the little man over the head with it. "Come on, out with it, or I'll kill you. Where are my diamonds?"

At that the man in the camel-hair coat intervened. "Stop it," he said, "there's no point. He really doesn't know."

"I think his wife knows. She left the Turkish cafe last night. I let her go because I wanted to keep an eye on Herr Civil. That was clearly a mistake. She's disposed of them."

"You're a dead loss," the fat man shouted. "I'm making you personally responsible. I'm giving you one more day, then you're for it."

He turned away slowly, plodded back to the limousine, and stopped halfway there. Several police vehicles with blue flashing lights turned off Hochbergerstrasse onto the fore-court and stopped. The doors opened and police leaped out, pistols at the ready.

The fat man put on his affable smile. He looked at the Browning in his hand and shook his head in disbelief. State Prosecutor Suter got out of the first car, along with Hunkeler and Madörin.

"Well, well," Suter said, "what a surprise. What are you doing here, Herr Dr Zeugin, if I may ask?"

"Oh, let's not bother with titles," fat Dr Zeugin said, still smiling as if he was delighted at the unexpected meet-ing. "What's in a title, they're just so much noise. Am I not right?"

"How right you are," Suter said, "but what do you intend to do with that pistol in your hand?"

"Good question," Dr Zeugin said, looking back at the other three men. "I have a problem here. Huber," he pointed at the bald man in handcuffs, "has strayed off the straight and narrow again. I've just relieved him of his pistol. Here, take it, I have a horror of weapons. And the other man there appears to be a Lebanese called Guy Kayat. I'm sure you know him. He does actually appear to be a criminal."

Kayat, also in handcuffs, made a polite bow. Then he had a furious coughing fit.

"And this poor little man here," Dr Zeugin went on, "appears to be a Turk called Erdogan Civil."

He pointed at Erdogan, who was being treated by a paramedic.

"This Turk," he went on with his explanation, "does appear to know something about the diamonds which you," he said, turning politely to Hunkeler, "were apparently looking for at Badischer Station. I did hear some mention of diamonds. Now just you look at this poor thing, how they've beaten him up. That's international crime. Those are the methods of the mafia. It's high time you got rid of these gangsters, Herr Suter, after all, you are the public prosecutor. And you," he said to Huber, "what are you doing going round with this criminal riffraff? You're ruining my name, my reputation. I'm deeply disappointed in you. I have no option but to dismiss you without notice."

Dr Zeugin put his hand over his heart, as if suddenly overcome. He was almost crying with disappointment and grief.

"Right then," Hunkeler said, "that's enough of the play-acting. You're arrested. Let's put the handcuffs on."

"And you just allow this to happen," Dr Zeugin said,

watching the two iron rings snap shut round his wrists. "You're allowing a respectable citizen with no previous convictions to be led off in handcuffs, my dear Suter?"

Suter had a sour look on his face. "I'm sorry to say that things don't look good for you." And then to Hunkeler, "Do what you have to."

He turned away, depressed, irresolute, went to the car, sat down in the back and waited.

"This will not be good for you, my friend," Dr Zeugin shouted after him, "you're going to regret it. I'll personally make sure of that."

"Shut your gob," Madörin barked, "and come along."

"I've nothing," Dr Zeugin said, "to say to you. You have a filthy imagination."

He let himself be led away with no further objections.

Hunkeler went over to Erdogan Civil, who was sitting on one of the steps to the changing room. He had a bandage round his head.

"He has a cut, not very deep, on his head," the paramedic said, "his left eyebrow is torn, his upper left canine has been knocked out. Added to that are various bruises. All in all he's been lucky."

"Does he need to be taken to hospital?" Hunkeler asked.

"That would be best. At least to be examined. And his eyebrow needs to be stitched."

"No," Erdogan said. "I'm not going to hospital. I'm going home to Erika."

"If he doesn't want to," the paramedic said, "it's not absolutely necessary."

Erdogan shook his head. "I'm as healthy as a horse, those are just scratches and bumps."

"Fix his eyebrow up as well as you can," Hunkeler said. "It'll grow together again."

He got up off the step, lit a cigarette, inhaling the smoke deeply. He rubbed his chin, it was scratchy. He badly needed a shave. He looked up at the sky. It was a real spring sky and it was only February. Some crows flew past, big black birds who were heading back into the woods.

"There's just one thing I'd like to ask you," he said. "Do you really have no idea where the diamonds are?"

"No," Erdogan said, "and I swear that on my mother's life."

Erika Waldis dragged the bags and suitcase up the stairs to her apartment. She had to stop several times and take a deep breath, it was such a heavy load. Climbing over walls, she thought, fleeing to France as the Holy Family fled to Egypt. Buying a vintage car and watching it being demolished in the middle of the night. Going back to Basel by taxi as if they were millionaires. Sleeping the afternoon away on a bench in a Turkish cafe, her ears full of foreign music. Flushing diamonds down her friend's toilet. Then watching her man being beaten up and abducted. And now having to drag this stupid suitcase halfway round Basel. And why all this bother? Because he's crazy. Because he's dreaming of immense wealth. Because he thinks he's Memed the Hawk.

But enough was enough. The adventures were over and that was that. Carefully wiping her shoes on the mat outside the door, she opened it and went in.

The apartment had been searched, she could see that at once. She wasn't surprised, she'd expected it. At least they'd made an effort to put most things back in their place.

She went to the aquarium and scattered some food in it. The goldfish came up immediately and started to eat. It must be hungry. One of the water plants had been moved. So they'd been looking there as well, in the black sand.

Once she'd taken off her coat and boots she put the kettle on to make coffee. The special-offer salmon she threw in the bucket, it was going off. The white loaf she kept to make bread soup. She opened a tin of tuna and emptied it onto a plate, added some slices of onion and poured a few drops of vinegar over it. Then she fetched the jar of capers from the fridge and ate standing up.

She had done the right thing, she was sure of that now. Erdogan would stay here, here with her in this apartment. He'd have to, he had no choice. And they'd go to Magliaso over Easter.

She was peeling carrots for vegetable soup when there was a ring at the door. She went and opened it. Erdogan came in, his face battered and bruised, a bandage round his head, a stitch in his left eyebrow. Behind him was Inspector Hunkeler.

Erika, alarmed, went to embrace Erdogan. He pushed her away, went over to the sofa and sat down. All without a word.

Hunkeler was visibly embarrassed. "I don't want to be a nuisance," he said. "I'll only stay for a moment. May I sit down?"

"Go ahead," Erika said, going into the kitchen and reappearing with the coffee pot and cups.

Hunkeler stroked his chin. "I stink to high heaven," he said, "I need to take a shower. May I smoke?"

He lit up, puffed out the smoke and coughed.

"I suspected," he said, "that the diamonds would be in the black sand, over there in the aquarium. I was wrong, they weren't there."

"No," Erika said.

She gave him a friendly smile. She was a charming hostess, a lady.

"Where are they now?" Hunkeler asked.

"They're back down in the sewers, where he found them. We don't need any diamonds."

Erdogan groaned. He felt his head, then his mouth. "There's a tooth missing," he wailed, "and it bloody hurts, the hole."

"Top left at the back?" Hunkeler asked.

Erdogan tried to grin but couldn't manage it. He groaned again.

"They were in his locker in the changing room," Erika said, "until yesterday evening. You'd already searched there. That was a cunning trick of his."

"The plastic bag on the moped luggage rack," Hunkeler said. "Arsehole that I am."

"I got them yesterday evening and flushed them down my friend's toilet."

"Why?" Hunkeler asked.

"Because I didn't want them to find the diamonds. They'd have killed him then because he'd seen their faces."

Hunkeler nodded and finished his coffee, apparently enjoying it very much.

"It could be that you're right there." He ran his hand over his chin, it was as scratchy as a birch broom. "And then you called us."

"Yes."

"Good. That'll all be put on your witness statement and you'll have to sign it. If you give false testimony you'll be liable to prosecution."

"I can swear to it on my mother's life," Erika said calmly. "Is she still alive?"

"Yes, in Weggis. We're going to see her at Easter."

He stood up. "Right then. Take good care of your man. We'll keep you informed." He went to the door. "By the way, just one more question. How many diamonds did you flush down the toilet? Did you count them?"

'No," she said without hesitation, "I simply emptied out the plastic bag."

"That's another problem solved then. Goodbye."

He went out.

Erika sat down on the sofa beside Erdogan and took his hand.

"I'm a broken man," he said, "tooth broken, head broken, car broken and money all gone."

"Things will get better," she said, "just you wait. I'll pay for all that, I've been saving up. I'll pay for the dentist if you want."

"No," he said, "no dentist, it hurts enough as it is. Strong as a horse, how stupid can you be? Weak as a dog, that's the sad truth."

She stood up, went to the door and listened.

"What are you doing?" he asked. "He's long since gone. He believed you because you told him the truth."

She opened the door, looked out. There was no one on the stairs. She squatted down, lifted up the doormat, retrieved something from underneath it and came back in. She sat in the armchair opposite him and put two glittering diamonds with a bluish shimmer on the table.

He gaped, looking at her in disbelief, then tried to grin. Things were already looking up.

"Where did you get those from?"

"Those are the two we were going to sell to the jeweller," she said. "Aren't they beautiful? That one's for you and this one's for me."